THE STRIKING LONE STAR TEAM MOVED QUICKLY THROUGH THE CROWDED TRAIN . . .

They were almost to the private coach when suddenly a pair of matched giants wearing deputy badges began to beat four shackled prisoners. The prisoners cringed and tried to protect themselves, and it was then that Jessie realized their faces were already badly swollen, cut and disfigured.

"Stop that!" Jessie shouted, pushing past Ki. "Stop it at once!"

The two brutes twisted around, and when they saw Jessie and the samurai, they sneered and unloaded a few more sledging blows to the faces of the men under their guard.

Jessie reached into her pocket and withdrew a handgun.

"If you hit those prisoners just once more, I'll shoot your fists off. What's it to be?"

The two giants gaped. "Miss," one of them rumbled, "you better put that little gun away before I come over there and— "

"You come a step closer," Jessie said, "and I'll do mankind a favor by just blowing a hole in your head."

*   *   *

SPECIAL PREVIEW!

Turn to the back of this book for a sneak-peek excerpt from the exciting, brand new Western series . . .

FURY

. . . the blazing story of a gunfighting legend.

Also in the LONE STAR series from Jove

WESLEY ELLIS

LONE STAR

AND THE
SANTA FE SHOWDOWN

J

JOVE BOOKS, NEW YORK

LONE STAR AND THE SANTA FE SHOWDOWN

A Jove Book / published by arrangement with
the author

PRINTING HISTORY
Jove edition / August 1992

ISBN: 0-515-10902-9

Jove Books are published by The Berkley Publishing Group,
200 Madison Avenue, New York, New York 10016.
The name "JOVE" and the "J" logo
are trademarks belonging to Jove Publications, Inc.

PRINTED IN THE UNITED STATES OF AMERICA

10 9 8 7 6 5 4 3 2 1

LONE STAR

AND THE
SANTA FE SHOWDOWN

Chapter 1

Jessie and Ki vaulted from the carriage and grabbed their luggage as they prepared to rush toward the Sacramento train depot.

"Here, Miss Starbuck," the driver of their coach shouted, as he jumped down and tried to wrench the large suitcase from Jessie's hand. "A beautiful woman like you shouldn't ever have to carry her own luggage."

Jessie's grip on her bag remained firm. "I appreciate your concern, but I'm quite capable of carrying my luggage. Besides, we are late and I'm in a hurry."

"Aw, hell," the driver argued, tugging at the bag, "this train ain't never on time! I insist on helping you!"

"You could have helped us by delivering us here on time instead of picking us up late."

"Now, ma'am," the driver said, his voice hardening, "I told you that one of the wheels was loose and the hub needed tightening. Ain't my fault. Now give me this here bag and I'll make it up to you."

The Central Pacific locomotive blasted a shrill call, and

1

Jessie saw the conductor cup his hands to his mouth and call, "All aboard!"

"We're going to miss that train!" Jessie said with exasperation.

"Not if you give me the damned bag!" the driver argued, the smell of whiskey heavy on his breath.

Jessie glanced at her best friend, protector, and traveling companion, the samurai. "Ki?"

Ki nodded. He stepped forward, and his hand locked on the driver's wrist. "Miss Starbuck said to let go."

The driver was a large, powerfully built young man. He snarled something as the train's whistle blasted again and the conductor jumped onto the landing platform. As the train jolted forward, Ki's fingers bit into flesh.

"Hey, damn you!"

"Jessie, catch the train," Ki said as the driver grabbed him in a bear hug and tried to wrestle him to the ground.

Jessie nodded and snatched up her fallen luggage. She was long legged, and as she raced toward the departing train, her honey-blond hair flashed in the sun with the glint of copper. Spectators and employees of the Central Pacific standing on the passenger loading dock watched with admiration as Jessie sprinted forward, grabbed a steel bar and leapt aboard the train as it gathered speed. They burst into applause, and Jessie waved as her green eyes saw Ki use a hip throw to fell the belligerent driver. The man grabbed the samurai's leg and twisted him to the earth. The two men rolled over and over, punching and kicking, each attempting to gain the superior position.

"Hurry!" Jessie cried, knowing that her words could never be heard over the sound of the train. The samurai managed to get on top. Jessie saw Ki's hand flash downward like the blade of a descending ax. It connected at the base of the driver's neck. The big man went limp,

2

allowing Ki to grab his satchel of clothes and weapons. The train was now a quarter mile to the east of the station and quickly gathering speed as the samurai dashed after it. The crowd departed, staring at the unusual man dressed in a black, loose-fitting outfit and wearing sandals instead of boots or even shoes. They could see that he was intent on overtaking the departing train, but it seemed impossible except perhaps on the back of a fast horse.

The samurai shot across the loading and passenger docks and left them, flying through the air. He landed in stride and sprinted along the railroad tracks. Even though the bag in his hand was large and cumbersome, he seemed to float effortlessly as he swiftly overtook the train and jumped on board.

Many in the crowd cheered again, but their applause was drowned by the locomotive's whistle as the train began to assault the high Sierras on its way over Donner Pass.

Jessie hugged the samurai. "I thought I was going to have to jump in another minute or two. I'd not have gone on without you, Ki."

"That man was strong and he wouldn't let go of my tunic," Ki said, his breath coming fast. "And cinders were soft and made running a little more difficult than I'd expected."

"You looked as fast as always," Jessie said. "I guess all that running that you do to keep in shape really pays off sometimes."

Ki nodded and gazed out at Sacramento, which was rapidly fading in the distance. "The driver was drunk but he was tough."

Jessie took the samurai's arm. "Let's go settle into that private coach that I was promised," Jessie said. "I've plenty of paperwork to keep me occupied from here to Cheyenne and I'm sure that you can find something exciting to do until we arrive."

"I've had enough excitement for one day," Ki said, taking Jessie's suitcase and starting forward. Jessie's private coach had been offered by the management of the Union Pacific Railroad because she was one of their most valued clients and also one of their major stockholders.

The train was crowded with passengers, many of them rough miners bound for Reno and then the Comstock Lode. They were hard, bold men who had worked in the mines and saved up their hard-earned wages in order to blow them on a spree at San Francisco's infamous Barbary Coast. But there were also ranchers, drummers, freighters, and a scattering of women and children.

The women and children were all located together in one of the better passenger cars, where several big railroad employees armed with batons and pistols kept order and made sure that the women were not subjected to any physical or verbal abuse by the mostly inebriated crowd.

As Ki swiftly led the way down the aisle and through the rougher sections of the train, several men tried to block his path in order to get a better look at Jessie. Each of these men learned a painful lesson as the samurai used his martial arts skills to render them helpless. Most amazing to those who had never encountered an oriental arts master was the way Ki applied *atemi*, the ancient and very effective use of pressure points to almost instantly render an opponent unconscious. To a casual observer, it appeared as if Ki merely touched a man and he dropped as if shot.

They were almost to the private coach when suddenly a pair of matched giants wearing deputy badges began to beat four shackled prisoners. The prisoners cringed and tried to protect themselves, and it was then that Jessie realized their faces were already badly swollen, cut and disfigured.

4

"Stop that!" Jessie shouted, pushing past Ki. "Stop it at once!"

The two brutes twisted around, and when they saw Jessie and the samurai, they sneered and unloaded a few more sledging blows to the faces of the men under their guard.

Jessie reached into her coat pocket and drew a handgun.

"If you hit those prisoners just once more, I'll shoot your fists off. What's it to be!"

The two giants gaped. The four smaller men cowered and looked around to see who had intervened. Jessie had never seen such a brutal-looking pair as the two big men who now stared at her and the gun in her fist. They were both well over six feet tall and extremely powerful-looking. They had massive jaws, wore black beards, and their eyes were hot and as pitiless as those of a pair of wolves. They were filthy, and they smelled like the old buffalo hiders and bone scavengers Jessie remembered as a former scourge of the Texas Panhandle country.

"Miss," one of them rumbled, "you better put that little gun away before I come over there and shove it up your pretty ass and then pull the trigger."

The other deputy thought that comment exceedingly funny. He began to chortle and it sounded like rutting pig.

"You come a step closer," Jessie said, "and I'll do mankind a favor by just blowing a hole in your head."

The laughter died and it was replaced by contempt. One of the deputies said, "You just better mind your own business, ma'am. These four are convicted murderers and they don't need yours or anybody else's damned sympathy."

"Are you United States marshals, or what?"

"We're deputies," the other man said. "But we've been sworn in by the judge down in Santa Fe, New Mexico, to hunt down these four dogs and bring them back for trial."

"Mind if I see the judge's orders?" Jessie asked.

5

"As a matter of fact, we do. It's like Abe just told you, we are just doin' our duty."

"Your duty isn't to beat prisoners half to death," Jessie said angrily. "Look at them!"

"We'll be lookin' at 'em all the way back to Santa Fe," Abe growled. "We been lookin' for 'em nearly six months. These men are our prisoners. Now you had best get your pretty ass outa this coach!"

Ki stepped around Jessie. "I think that you'd better watch your language in Miss Starbuck's company."

The two giants broke into snickers. Finally, Abe said, "Chinaman, if you give me or Eli any more lip, we'll toss you right out the window. You hear me now?"

Ki started forward, but Jessie grabbed his arm and held him back. The aisle was small, and she knew that against such large and fierce men, Ki stood the chance of getting badly hurt in a fight. Also, in the small confines of this coach, the samurai's advantage of speed and mobility was severely restricted.

"Let's let this pass for now," Jessie said to her companion. "This train will lay over for a few hours in Reno. That will be enough time to contact the marshal and find out if these four prisoners are really wanted for murder."

"Don't meddle, woman," Abe warned in a hard voice. "It ain't healthy."

Again, Ki started forward, but Jessie's grip tightened on his arm. "Not now," she said.

Ki was trained to obedience. As a samurai, his life's purpose was to serve a master, and Jessie was his master. He did not always agree with her orders, but he was honor bound to carry them out, except when they put her life in danger. That being the case, he reluctantly nodded and slipped past the giants to continue down the aisle. As they passed, one of the prisoners whispered, "It ain't true!

6

None of what they told you is true, ma'am! You've got to help—"

His plea was abruptly punctuated by the sound of a fist striking flesh. The man cried out in pain and blood poured from a busted nose.

Jessie drew her pistol, cocked back the hammer and said, "If you strike *any* of those men again, I'll have you arrested in Reno! I'll hire the best lawyer money can buy and have you both sentenced to the Nevada State Prison. Is that understood!"

The two giants towered over her, spilling hatred. Abe said, "Woman, you are steppin' into something you should have never troubled yourself about."

"Maybe," Jessie said, her green eyes flicking down to the face of the man whose nose had just been broken and who was now covered with blood. "But I wouldn't stand by and watch you treat an animal the way you've been treating these men. And I am going to make sure that it stops!"

This time it was the samurai who had to physically restrain Jessie and then gently guide her on to their private coach. It was luxurious and boasted velvet wallpaper, rich mahogany furniture and expensive oil paintings. A black porter stood by to serve their every need.

"George, please bring me a stiff drink," Jessie said, flopping down on a couch and feeling her insides still quaking with anger.

George had often served Jessie and the samurai on their frequent trips either to or from Sacramento on this train, and he knew exactly what Jessie required, and also that she would tip him extravagantly when the journey ended in Cheyenne.

"What kind of men are those deputies from New Mexico?" Jessie asked, looking up at Ki. "I couldn't stand by and watch them mistreat those four prisoners. I don't care what crimes

7

they might have committed—they are still human beings."

Ki nodded. He had been with Jessie long enough to know that she could not tolerate cruelty in any form. "Did you mean what you said about asking the United States marshal in Reno to question those men?"

"You bet I did! Just as soon as the train stops, we are going to find him and get some answers."

"And if they really are deputized?"

"I can't believe they are!"

Ki persisted. "But if they are and if the four men they have handcuffed really are murderers, what then?"

Jessie shook her head. "You know that I believe in swift justice."

"I know."

"But I also believe that punishment should be meted out by *the courts*, not by a couple of sadistic deputies. Ki, those men are totally unfit to be given the power of the law which they are abusing!"

George arrived with Jessie's drink. She took a long swallow, settled back on the couch and stared out at the passing forest. Their train was now in the foothills of the western Sierra Nevada Mountains, and it would be a long, winding ascent to the summit of Donner Pass. An ascent that would take all day and half the night. But tomorrow, by noon, they would be rushing down the eastern slopes of these great mountains into Nevada and their first stop would be in Reno.

"Something just isn't right here," Jessie said. "And I'll tell you another thing—if we don't watch out, those four will never live to stand trial in New Mexico."

"How can you be so sure?"

Jessie took another drink. "Call it woman's intuition. Call it something a lot stronger than a hunch—call it what you want, but I saw something terrible in the eyes of those two men when they were using their fists on their prisoners. It was . . . it was pure hatred. Even stronger than hatred."

Jessie heaved a sigh. "Those four are dead men if something isn't done to see that they reach trial in New Mexico."

Ki nodded with agreement. Like Jessie, he was a pretty good judge of character, and he'd read it just as she had—without help and protection the four prisoners were walking dead men who would never live to see a trial.

Chapter 2

The rest of that afternoon and evening, Jessie and Ki remained in their private coach as the train slowly crawled up the western slopes of the rugged Sierra Nevada Mountains. Jessie could not look out her window without being reminded of the terrible sacrifices made by the Chinese coolies who had picked and blasted this hard-won railroad bed over the mountains. They had encountered terrible snows near Donner Summit, and when they'd had to burrow under it, they'd spent endless months of hardship buried in snow caves under the snow and rocks. Hundreds of Chinese had been buried alive or had died of pneumonia or other accidents before summit tunnels had been completed, allowing the Central Pacific to follow along the Truckee River down to Reno.

Dinner was superb—roast pheasant under glass garnished with a wonderful apricot sauce, delicately steamed carrots, wild rice, and apple pie for dessert.

"I should be doing paperwork," Jessie said after dessert, "but I can't stop thinking about those two deputies and their abused prisoners."

10

"Should I go see how they are doing?" Ki asked.

"Would you?" Jessie asked. "But don't let them crowd you into a fight. Just take a look. Act like you are passing through their coach and, if you can, ask the conductor if he has any specifics about those prisoners."

"Such as?"

Jessie shrugged her shoulders. "Their names. The crimes they are accused of committing. How they were captured. You know, that sort of thing."

Ki understood, and as he was moving toward the door, Jessie couldn't help but offer one last warning. "Those two men are vicious, Ki. I know that you have complete confidence in the art of hand fighting, in *te*, but I'd still feel more comfortable if you'd at least take the *nunchaku*."

He nodded. "Good idea."

Ki went over to his bag and removed the *nunchaku*. It was two sticks attached to each other by a few inches of braided horsehair. The one Ki selected was his favorite, a half-sized version called a *han-kei*. The two sticks were about seven inches long and flat on one side so that they fit smoothly together. With this weapon, Ki could effectively perform virtually every *te* block and strike, but with the additional power brought to bear by the terrible centrifugal force generated when the *han-kei* began to whirl.

Jessie had seen this ancient weapon used by Ki on several occasions, and it was frightening to behold. With the *han-kei*, the samurai could easily smash an opponent's face or throat. He could also crush an enemy's bones between the two sticks as easily as if they were walnuts in a nutcracker.

"Maybe I should come along," Jessie offered.

"I would prefer to do it alone."

"All right. But if you are not back within an hour, I'll come looking for you with a gun."

11

Ki smiled. "I am supposed to be the one that protects *you*, remember?"

"Friends protect each other," Jessie reminded.

Ki knew that it was absolutely futile to argue with Jessie. She had been raised to speak her own mind, and like her father, the late Alex Starbuck, she was quite decisive and opinionated. Jessie's father had not built a worldwide empire of factories, ranches, mines, plantations and railroads by being shy, and his daughter was cut of exactly the same cloth.

"I'll be back within an hour," Ki vowed. "And as for those two 'deputies,' I wouldn't worry about them."

"How could I *not* be worried?" Jessie asked. "They've the look of killers, not lawmen. And that poor man who had his nose broken! They all looked as if they needed the services of a doctor."

"I'll ask the conductor if there is a doctor on board," Ki promised. "And if that pair refuse to allow their prisoners to be examined, then I'll just have to convince them that they need to be more humane."

"Then," Jessie said with a knowing smile, "*they* will be the ones that will need medical attention."

Ki did not deny that possibility as he slipped the *han-kei* under the waistband of his black tunic and left the coach to begin his investigation.

When he entered the coach where the bounty hunters and their four prisoners were being held, Abe looked up at him with hate in his black eyes. "You come looking for trouble again, Chinaman? This time, you ain't got little fancy pants to protect you."

"I'm not a Chinaman," Ki said very quietly, "and I don't need anyone's protection."

"Yeah?" Abe stood up. He towered over Ki. "Well, if you don't need protectin' from me, then it can't snow on

Donner Pass, you yellow pissant!"

Ki stood his ground calmly. He would respect Jessie's orders to avoid trouble if possible. He would, however, be ready to defend himself if this brutish and cruel man tried to get rough. At that moment, however, the conductor entered the coach. When he saw the look on the giant's face, he rushed down the aisle. "Is there some problem here, Ki?"

"Nothing I can't take care of," the samurai said, not taking his eyes off the big deputy.

The conductor was a large Irishman named O'Brien who had once been an excellent bare knuckles fighter, until age and a watermelon gut had convinced him that his best days were gone. Even so, he could still be intimidating, and he wasn't one bit afraid of the New Mexico deputies.

"You gentlemen had better sit down and relax," O'Brien said, stepping between Ki and the giant. "I think that it would be best for all concerned if you just took your seats, gentlemen."

"Don't push me, bub," Abe warned. "If you do, I'll shove your fat Irish ass out the window and this Chinaman will be right behind."

O'Brien bristled and his fists balled at his sides. "So, you're threatening me now, are ye! Is that what it is!"

Ki gently placed his hand on O'Brien's broad shoulder. "It's all right, Conductor. I was just passing through and we had a little personal disagreement. That's all."

O'Brien backed off a little. His face was flushed with anger, and it was clear that he wanted to take a swing at Abe, the consequences to his health and his job be damned.

"The agent in Sacramento must have been daft to sell you men tickets!" O'Brien growled. "But since he did, you've got a right to stay on this train just as long as you behave yourselves. Misbehave, and I'll see that your

13

money is refunded and you are tossed off at the next stop. You understand me!"

"Shove it!" Eli growled.

O'Brien shook like a water spaniel after a swim. It was all that Ki could do to restrain the conductor.

"Why don't we go find ourselves a cup of coffee?" Ki suggested. "I think that Miss Starbuck would enjoy seeing you again, Mr. O'Brien."

The Irishman allowed himself to be pulled back from Abe and Eli but not before he looked at the prisoners and shook his head with disgust. "I don't know what the world is comin' to when they give animals the authority of the law. Are you men all right?"

"Hell no, we ain't!" one of the men whimpered. "We'll never live to see Santa Fe!"

"If they were going to do that," Ki said, "why didn't they do it when you were captured? Why buy you tickets on this train for Cheyenne?"

Abe shoved in between Ki and the prisoners. "We done explained that already. We're deputies come to take these men to Santa Fe for trial."

"That's what *they* say!" one of the prisoners wailed. "The truth is, they need to keep us alive in order to get us to deed over our family's ranch."

"Hell!" Eli snorted. "All you Lane brothers got is some dirt-poor land covered with sagebrush and a few scrub pine. Ain't worth nothin' near what our land is worth. Why, we wouldn't take your damned ranch if you up and gave the worthless son of a bitch to us outright!"

"Worthless!" The prisoner scoffed. "You need our water rights. With a drought two years runnin' in that high mountain country, your ranch is dryin' up and blowin' away. Your streams are runnin' dry and your grass is the color of dried wheat. In a few more years, we'll own your ranch!"

14

Ki stared at Abe and Eli. "You're also brothers?"

"What the hell of it!" Eli snapped. "We're both deputies. Ain't nothing unusual about deputizin' a pair of brothers that knows how to catch skunks!"

"You may manage to kill us all," one of the prisoners choked. "But Pa and the women, they ain't never going to give up the homestead. Never!"

Abe drew back his fist, but before he could smash his prisoner, both Ki and the Irishman stepped in between. "You touch them in my presence," O'Brien warned, his voice trembling, "and by the authority vested in me, I'll have you arrested and put in irons! And when we reach Reno, you'll be brought before the law and charged according to federal railroad law! You'll go to prison, by damn!"

Abe lowered his fist. "Conductor," he whispered, "you have brought yourself a heap more grief than you can imagine. Me and my brother ain't likely to forget the way you took their sides over that of the law."

"Good!" O'Brien whirled around to Ki. "Now why don't you and I go visit Miss Starbuck?"

"Yes," Ki said, "let's do that."

They left the deputies and their prisoners and moved up the aisle. When they arrived at the special coach, Jessie poured the Irishman a tumbler of whiskey, and O'Brien tossed it down, smacked his lips and sighed.

"I could lose me job fighting with them sonsabitches," he said quietly. "I can't afford to do that."

"Then try not to let them bother you so much," Jessie said. "Ki and I will watch them closely."

"That's right," Ki said, not wanting to see the Irishman come to any unnecessary grief. "If I see those two physically abusing their prisoners, then you can arrest them under . . . and they'll be tried under that . . . what did you call it?"

15

O'Brien grinned sheepishly. "A federal railroad law, or some such nonsense."

"You made it up?"

"I did," O'Brien admitted. "I have the authority to stop fights, arrest thieves, murderers and such, but only as a last resort. I don't even carry a gun. I'm not supposed to be a policeman, but I'm not afraid to protect my passengers from harm, even when they are prisoners."

"How were they captured?"

"I don't know," O'Brien said, extending his glass for more whiskey. "I heard that they were panning gold on the Feather River when the Hogan brothers caught them out in the stream without their weapons."

"That's their name, the Hogan brothers?"

"Aye," O'Brien growled. "And they are as evil a pair as I've ever laid eyes on. That's why I've put them in their own damn coach even though it meant I had to crowd some of the other passengers."

Jessie felt sorry for the conductor, and she could see that he was visibly upset. She told O'Brien about her plan to visit the United States marshal in Reno and see if he'd ever seen a Wanted poster on the four Lane brothers.

"Poster or not," the Irishman said, "those deputies need to carry some proof of their authority."

"We'll make sure that the marshal demands it in Reno," Jessie vowed "And if they haven't some sort of official authorization from a Santa Fe judge, then perhaps the marshal can intervene to save those prisoners."

"Those Hogan men won't hand over their prisoners without a fight," Ki said.

Jessie sighed. "I'm afraid I agree. Tell me, did you believe any of that talk about water rights?"

"It sounded pretty convincing," Ki said. "And I could tell the mention of water rights touched a sensitive nerve."

16

Jessie said, "We've got to keep a sharp watch on them or those four prisoners may not even live to see Reno."

"Agreed," Ki said quietly. "And as soon as it's dark, I'll sneak into their coach and keep a vigil."

"How are you going to do that without them seein' you?" O'Brien demanded.

"He is *ninja*," Jessie explained. "Ki can go anywhere he wants without being seen."

The Irishman didn't believe a word of it, but that didn't matter. Jessie did and so did the samurai.

★
Chapter 3

Ki stood atop the swaying railroad coach and tasted the sharp bite of the cold Sierra wind. The stars overhead shone like diamonds, and as the train labored up the mountainside, the heavy forest seemed to lean over the tracks, attempting to smother steam and smoke. In some places, tree branches actually scraped the sides of the passing coaches.

The samurai walked forward, in perfect balance with the swaying of the train. He transited one coach, then leapt across an eight-foot chasm onto the roof of another. Ki repeated this three times, and when he dropped down between the cars, he landed very softly. He then opened the door a crack and slipped inside to watch the Hogan brothers. As he was about to sneak into the deputies' coach, he heard a shout and a cry of pain. He stepped inside, but before he could move forward, Ki heard a second, louder scream.

"Ayyeei!"

The front door of the coach slammed shut and two shots were fired. Ki rushed forward in the darkness, certain the deputies were executing their prisoners. He slammed into a figure and was instantly embroiled in a fierce struggle. He was loath to use his *han-kei* because of the darkness.

In the chaos, he was felled, and when he tried to rise, someone tripped and fell on his outstretched left arm. Ki bit back a scream as he felt his arm snap. An orange light exploded behind his eyes and the samurai lost consciousness.

"Ki!" The words floated down to him and Ki struggled to answer. His lips moved soundlessly, and then he distinctly heard Jessie say, "Let's get him up to my private coach."

"What about. . . ."

"There's nothing more we can do for the prisoners now, Mr. O'Brien."

Ki had already recognized O'Brien's voice and knew the big Irishman who was lifting and carrying him up through the coaches. Ki struggled to speak, but his tongue felt thick and his vision was blurred. When he tried to raise his hand and help himself, he was shocked to discover that his limbs were numb. For the first time since becoming a man, Ki was frightened. Calm yourself, he thought. Something terrible has happened and you must gather all your resources.

"Ki," Jessie said, when he was resting on her bed, "can you hear me?"

He tried again to speak, and this time he heard his own voice. "Yes. What happened?"

Tears of relief rolled down Jessie's cheeks. "I was afraid that you'd suffered some terrible brain damage."

Ki stared at his discolored left arm. It had already been splinted and was badly bruised and swollen. "Did the bone break the skin?"

"No," Jessie told him. "At least for that we can be thankful."

Ki attempted to wiggle the fingers of his left hand. Nothing. He turned and studied the fingers of his right hand.

19

Index finger first—he willed it to move and it did. He wiggled the other fingers, but they moved slowly.

"Can you raise your right arm?" Jessie asked.

"I think so."

"Try."

Ki raised his arm, but it felt numb and seemed very heavy.

"What about your feet?" Jessie asked, looking down at his feet.

Ki wiggled the toes on his right foot, then his left.

"Raise your left leg."

He did, but it was heavy and unresponsive.

"Probably a concussion," O'Brien said solemnly. "I've seen 'em before when I used to be a fighter."

"It will pass, won't it?" Jessie managed to ask.

"Sure. Just takes time." O'Brien cleared his throat. "But I'm no doctor. I just seen it a few times is all."

Ki heard a catch in Jessie's throat and said, "I'm going to be fine. I just need rest."

"Of course!" She forced a smile. "When we get to Reno, we'll leave this train and find a hotel and the best doctor available. We'll stay there until . . ."

"No," Ki said softly. "I really don't want to stay in some hotel."

"But . . ."

"Jessie," Ki said, speaking slowly but very deliberately, "I can get better on this train just as easily as I can in a hotel room. And I'll be fine by the time that we are ready to depart in Cheyenne."

"But what—"

Ki lifted his right hand and touched her cheek. "And if I'm not, *then* we'll find a doctor. I promise I'll be all right."

"Of course you will!" Jessie said, trying to sound hopeful.

Ki turned his head toward O'Brien. He needed to know what had happened to the prisoners. "The Lane brothers. Are they still alive?"

O'Brien shook his head. "All hell must have broke loose in that coach. One of the brothers musta somehow gotten out of his handcuffs and tried to jump from the train. He didn't make it. He's lyin' over the coupling between the cars with a bullet in him. Another is shot in the shoulder. He might live and he might not."

"And the other two?"

"The Hogan brothers have them hogtied but they've taken an awful beating."

Ki shook his head. "We can't let this happen."

"What can I do!" O'Brien exclaimed. "They say that they're authorized to use any force necessary when their prisoners try to escape."

"We'll just see about that!" Jessie said hotly. "When this train gets to Reno, there'll be an accounting!"

But O'Brien was not so sure. "Miss Starbuck," he said, "the Central Pacific won't adjust its train schedule on account of this trouble. There's a westbound train that has to be handled on these tracks, too, you understand. That means we hold over for exactly two hours and then Jesus Christ himself couldn't talk the railroad officials into waiting any longer."

"Two hours," Jessie said, shaking her head. "I'd forgotten the time was so short."

"I'll do everything I can to help you," O'Brien promised, "but I am expected to remain on this train. I have to oversee the other employees, make sure that everything is replenished and that we are ready for the Nevada and Utah deserts. I can't go runnin' off looking for a doctor or a marshal."

"I understand," Jessie said quietly. "I'll just have to do it myself."

O'Brien looked very relieved to hear that. He smiled with encouragement. "Maybe one of the other passengers would be good enough to find a doctor for Ki along with the marshal."

"Thanks," Jessie said, "but I can't afford to depend on a stranger—not when lives are at stake."

O'Brien said, "Don't forget that we also need an undertaker."

"Yes," she said, her hands forming hard, angry knots. "I just wish that we had done something in Sacramento about those two men! If we had, we would have saved one life, possibly two."

"There is a chance that those four prisoners really are murderers," O'Brien said quietly.

"That doesn't matter a whit," Jessie argued. "They deserve a trial. That's what our country's legal system is founded upon. That's what justice is all about."

"Of course," O'Brien said, sounding contrite.

Jessie moved to the window. They were traveling down the eastern slopes of the Sierras, often under the huge snow sheds that had been devised by the engineers as the only possible method of keeping the tracks from being buried during frequent avalanches.

Far below, she could see the great desert basin and the little town of Reno. Jessie prayed that she would find a strong and forceful United States marshal to help her right the wrong that was taking place on this train. And if she did not, what then? What could she hope to do against men like the Hogan brothers? It was clear that they would not hesitate to ward off interference with their guns.

My first responsibility is to Ki, Jessie reminded herself. I must find the best doctor in town and bring him with me to examine the samurai. And if he believes that Ki should remain in Reno, then I have to abide with that decision

22

because Ki's life and health outweigh everything.

"Jessie?"

She turned to see Ki watching her closely.

"Jessie," he repeated, "I'm going to be fine and I'm not leaving this train."

"We'll see," she managed to say. "We'll just have to wait and see."

Chapter 4

Jessie made sure that she was the first person off the train. In fact, she didn't even wait for it to come to a complete halt before she jumped onto the station platform and hurried down Virginia Street. Reno had started out as an emigrant's crossing of the Truckee River and originally had been known as Lake's Crossing. The town was later renamed by the president of the Central Pacific Railroad, Charles Crocker, in honor of General Jesse Reno, a union officer killed by Indians a few years earlier. Reno soon became a distribution center for the fabulously wealthy mines on the Comstock Lode.

Now, except for the Comstock Lode itself, Reno could claim Nevada's largest population and was the undisputed center of its commerce, agriculture and banking. For all these reasons and more, Jessie was sure that she could find any number of qualified doctors to examine Ki and prescribe what was in his best interests. She was also quite sure that she could find a marshal who would take the matter of the poor Lane brothers into protective custody.

Her first concern was the doctor, and since she did not

want to merely go into the first office she stumbled across, Jessie rushed into the Northern Nevada Bank of Commerce, where she had previously done business and knew the manager, Mr. Applegate.

Fortunately, he was alone and came right out to see her. "Miss Starbuck, what a wonderful surprise!"

"I'm afraid not," she said, quickly explaining the purpose of her hurried visit. She ended by saying, "I don't know who else to ask for help."

Applegate was a tall, awkward man in his mid-forties. He was also intelligent and decisive, two qualities that Jessie most admired and sought in those who managed her worldwide Starbuck enterprises.

"I know just the right doctor for Ki," Applegate said, grabbing up his coat and hat and yelling at his office staff that he would be gone for a couple of hours.

Once outside, they hurried down the crowded boardwalk and Applegate talked very rapidly. "Dr. Evans is young and only just out of medical school, however—"

"I can't afford to use an inexperienced man," Jessie interrupted.

"But Dr. Evans graduated from the Harvard School of Medicine and when he arrived to assist Dr. Cline, he made it a point to tell me that he specialized in traumatic injuries—bullet wounds, head injuries, broken bones. I've heard he is excellent and very skilled."

"All right," Jessie said, "if you think he would be best."

"Definitely," Applegate said. "As you will understand, most frontier doctors have no formal education. What they know is what they've learned through books, trial and errors. That's not the kind of a doctor that you want."

"Of course not."

"Here," Applegate said, steering Jessie into a little office that bore Dr. Cline's name alone.

They were met by an older physician and Applegate quickly made the introductions. "We need your associate, Dr. Evans, to come to the train at once," Applegate explained. "There has been a gun battle and Miss Starbuck's dearest friend is injured."

"Well . . . well perhaps I should come myself," the older man said. "Things are a little slow today and I could close my office for a short while."

"No," Jessie said firmly, understanding the situation and in no mood to settle for anything but the best doctor that could be found. "I mean you no disrespect, but I insist that Dr. Evans care for my friend."

Dr. Cline's bushy eyebrows raised imperiously. "Well! In that case, you can step through the office and find him throwing horseshoes in the alley."

"Horseshoes?"

"Exactly," Dr. Cline said. "He is rather passionate about them and probably wins more money throwing horseshoes than he does practicing medicine."

Jessie glanced at Applegate, who smiled weakly and led the way down the hall and out the back door. Sure enough, there were four young, well-dressed businessmen pitching horseshoes. They all looked like merchants to Jessie, but it was clear that they'd been enjoying a spirited game up to the very moment they laid their eyes on her.

"Well, hello!" the tallest one said, removing his bowler and stepping forward with a pair of forgotten horseshoes clutched in his left hand. "Don't tell me that you need a doctor! I couldn't be *that* lucky."

"She looks very healthy to me!" another of the young men called.

Dr. Cline flushed with embarrassment. "Not very professional, Edward."

Edward's smile slipped badly. "I'm sorry."

Jessie was not in a mood to be charmed, even by a man as handsome as Dr. Edward Evans. Very quickly, she catagorized Ki's injuries and that of the wounded prisoner.

Dr. Evans, to his credit, listened until she was finished, and by then the other players had grown somber. Evans dropped his horseshoes and wiped the dirt off his hands before he said, "I need my medical bag and then we can leave."

Jessie looked to the banker. "If you would be so kind, would you round up your marshal and send him over to the train?"

"I'm afraid that he is out of town," Applegate said, looking apologetic.

Jessie tried to hide her acute disappointment, but failed. "There must be *someone* who has the authority to confront those deputies."

The banker and physican exchanged glances and said nothing, prompting Jessie to exclaim, "Well, isn't there!"

"We have a sheriff," Applegate hedged.

"Fine! Then tell him to please—"

"But he isn't much of a sheriff, Miss Starbuck. In fact, some of us have been trying to get rid of him for the past year."

"What's wrong with him?"

"Oh," Evans said, "just about anything you can think of. He's corrupt, inept and worthless." The doctor looked to the banker. "Did I forget anything?"

"No," Applegate said, "I think you've pretty well covered his most obvious shortcomings."

"Wonderful," Jessie said with exasperation. "Well, I don't care. If he's wearing a badge, perhaps we can shame or coerce him into fulfilling his duty."

"Who are the prisoners?"

"Their names are Lane," Jessie said. "And they are from around Santa Fe, New Mexico. Before the sheriff arrives, it might serve him well to quickly look through his Wanted posters and see if they are actually being sought by the New Mexico authorities."

"All right," the banker said, sounding very skeptical about the entire affair, "but I wouldn't pin my hopes on the sheriff finding anything. His office is, to put it mildly, in an advanced state of disarray."

"Wonderful!" Jessie said angrily. "Just perfect! Without help, the other prisoners are almost certain to be killed before they ever have a chance to defend themselves in a New Mexico court of law."

"I'm sorry," Applegate said, "but there is nothing else to be done."

Jessie knew the man was right, but it galled her terribly. A short time later, when Jessie and Dr. Evans returned to the train, they went straight to Jessie's private car. Ki was resting easily and O'Brien was trying to keep him company.

Dr. Evans was all business when he began to examine the samurai. The first thing he did was to study his pupils closely for several seconds. "Uh-huh."

He next examined the broken arm. Glancing at Jessie, he said, "Did you splint this?"

"Yes."

Evans removed the splint and gently began to examine the arm, using a delicate touch. "You both did a very good job," Evans said at last. "The bone is cracked, not broken. It should mend quickly."

"Thanks be to God," the conductor said, expelling a deep breath.

"What about his head wound?" Jessie asked.

"Obviously a concussion," Evans told her, opening his

28

medical kit and producing a needle, which he quickly threaded with gut. "This is going to hurt enough to warrant some laudanum, Ki."

"No thanks."

"Are you sure?"

"Yes."

"All right. Grab ahold of the edge of the bed and don't be embarrassed to change your mind."

"I can't grip with my left hand."

"I see. Well, that is only temporary, I promise you. All you need is rest."

"We're going on to Cheyenne," Ki said. "I won't hold everything up by staying here."

"It would be better if you did," Evans said.

"Then that's what we will do," Jessie decided.

Ki wanted to argue, but it was not his place, especially in front of a stranger.

"All right," the doctor said, "let's get this laceration sutured." When the needle pierced his flesh, Ki had already put his mind away in a distant place. He felt the pain, but he also felt detached and he did not flinch.

"It must be numb around the point of injury," the doctor said, "or else he would be squirming."

"Not Ki," Jessie said. "He has the ability to push pain from his mind."

"Oh really?"

The doctor did not believe it. She could see that he did not, even though Ki was totally relaxed.

About the time that Dr. Evans was finished with the suturing, a knock sounded at the door. "Mr. O'Brien, would you please see who that is?"

The Irishman went to the door. Jessie heard hushed whispers, and then the conductor closed the door and came back to Jessie. "It's the sheriff of Reno."

29

Jessie nodded. "Ki, I'll be back soon. I have to take care of this matter now."

The samurai wanted to protest, to tell Jessie that she needed him if she were going to confront the Hogan brothers again. But Jessie was already leaving, and Ki knew he was in no condition to do anything but mend.

★

Chapter 5

"My name," the chubby, buck-toothed man said, "is Sheriff Ted Roach. I understand that you've got a problem."

"A problem? You call one man having been shot to death, his brother wounded and my friend's skull cracked open 'a problem'!"

Roach blinked. "Well, this is the frontier, Miss. . . ."

"Starbuck! Jessica Starbuck. And we've a lot more than 'a problem' on this train."

"Well, that's what I'm here for," he said, smiling weakly.

Jessie tried to hide her disappointment. Sheriff Roach was big, but so fat and sloppy-looking that it was impossible not to judge him rather harshly. He had a wispy blond mustache and a ridiculous little goatee, waxed at the tips. His clothes were dirty and even his badge had lost its shine.

Jessie shut the door behind her. "Let me get right to the point of your visit," Jessie said. "There are two brothers on this train that claim they have been deputized by a judge in Santa Fe, New Mexico. The Hogans insist they have lawfully arrested four brothers for murder."

31

"Two brothers arrested four brothers?" Roach asked, frowning with concentration.

"That's right," Jessie said. "And the Hogans have already shot two of the prisoners. One died and is still awaiting the undertaker. The second has a bullet in his shoulder which Dr. Evans will try to remove very soon."

Jessie paused for a response, and the sheriff finally said, "What exactly am I supposed to do? If the two brothers are deputized, they got the right to shoot escaping prisoners."

"How could they have been escaping with all of them handcuffed together! And them on a train going over the Sierras!"

"I'll admit it wouldn't be all that easy."

Jessie curbed her impatience with this slow-witted oaf. She could not help but wonder how in heaven's name he had ever gotten elected to the position of sheriff. It must have been a rigged or a bought election, not uncommon in the West, where a candidate with enough ready cash to buy whiskey votes usually emerged as the victor.

"Why don't we go and see if we can get to the bottom of this?" Jessie suggested when the man showed no signs of offering to take action.

Sheriff Roach nodded without enthusiasm. "Why sure. I can at least talk to them."

Jessie's heart sank. "I'll expect a damn sight more than that," she said, trying to keep her voice under control.

Roach looked away, and when he would not meet her eyes, Jessie knew that this was going to be an exercise in futility. However, she hoped that bringing a lawman into the picture might at least have the effect of a warning to the Hogan brothers that they would be held accountable to the law if there was any more shooting.

It took them only a few minutes to reach the coach containing the prisoners and their captors. Jessie had not

32

seen the dead brother or the wounded one until now, and the sight was rather unnerving. The dead man was sitting up in one of the seats, head jammed between the seat and the window, eyes staring vacantly up at the ceiling. The wounded brother was lying in the aisle, his face ashen with pain. The other two brothers were cowering in a seat, too unnerved to take their eyes off the deputies.

"Just what the hell do you want!" Abe demanded. "I won't brook any interference."

"Distraction!" Jessie cried. "Can you explain to me or the sheriff how the prisoners could possibly have attempted an escape while all handcuffed together?"

Abe and Eli looked over at Sheriff Roach; they had sized him up as a weakling at first glance. "Sheriff," Abe said, "speakin' as one lawman to another, you know that a prisoner facin' the gallows will try damn near any foolish thing he can to escape the hangman's rope."

"That is true," Roach said, dipping his double chins vigorously.

"And it is also true," Abe continued, "that sometimes, in the dark, things can get out of hand with a man . . . or a woman."

When he said that, his eyes locked on Jessie's bosom, and she flushed with anger and humiliation.

"Show him papers to prove you have the authority to arrest these men!" Jessie demanded.

"Hell," Eli drawled, "we ain't got no papers! What good would they do us anyway, we cain't even read nor write!"

Abe giggled childishly. "That's a fact, Sheriff Roach. Neither one of us can read nor write. So a paper wouldn't mean a thing. Could be a shoppin' list for all we'd know."

"That's right," Eli said, looking very proud of himself.

"Well what about a Wanted poster!" Jessie demanded. "At least you need that much before you can just take men hostage and then shoot and mistreat them."

"A Wanted poster?"

"That's right!" Jessie turned on the sheriff. "I demand that they show us a Wanted poster!"

Roach squirmed under the hard looks of Abe and Eli and cleared his throat. He shuffled his feet and scratched his ponderous belly.

Jessie's temper broke. "Well, Sheriff! Are you at least going to demand Wanted posters!"

Roach gulped. Without meeting the Hogan brothers in the eye, he mumbled, "You got 'em, boys?"

"Hell no!" Abe stormed. "We couldn't read them any better than we could the other thing!"

Both brothers cackled at their little joke, and they made Jessie want to vomit. Instead, she said, "Well the least you can do, Sheriff, is to check your own files to see if there are any outstanding Wanted posters on the Lane brothers."

"That's their names?" Roach asked, looking down at the dead and wounded brothers with morbid curiosity.

"That's right!" Jessie said. "Now will you at least do that much! And if you don't find anything on them, then I'm going to insist that those men are removed from this train and placed in your protective custody until the United States Marshal returns to Reno."

"He won't want to fuss with 'em any more'n I do," Roach said. "We got more than enough troubles all by ourselves without addin' any outside fusses."

Jessie wanted to tear the man's face with her fingernails. Instead, she gripped the door and said, "Go look through your Wanted posters and see if you can confirm that the Lane brothers are really fugitives of the law."

"Yes, ma'am. But . . . but the train won't wait on me. It'll be leavin' in an hour."

"Then hurry!"

Roach left the train, and Jessie watched him shuffle across the loading platform as if he were on his way to a funeral.

"I got a real strong feelin' that that Sheriff Roach ain't comin' back, don't you, Abe?" Eli said with a smirk.

"I sure do!"

They both grinned maliciously at Jessie, and she was about to leave when Dr. Evans and O'Brien appeared. The doctor wasted no time but went right to the wounded man's side. He tore the bloodied shirt away and called for some water to cleanse the wound.

Water was brought immediately, and when the doctor probed the wound, the man on the floor screamed. Dr. Evans glanced up. "This man needs to be hospitalized."

"He ain't goin' nowheres," Abe Hogan growled. "You want to take the slug outa his shoulder, you're going to have to do it right here. If Nate dies, you can haul his ass off the train and bury him beside his worthless, murderin' brother. But if he lives — well, Doc—if he lives he's going to stand trial for murder in old Santa Fe along with his brothers."

"All right," Evans said tightly. "I'll remove the slug right here on the floor. Miss Starbuck, I may need your assistance if you are up to it."

"Of course."

For the next ten minutes, Dr. Evans worked very swiftly and skillfully as he probed the wound and finally managed to grip the lead slug with his forceps.

"I'll clean the wound and we'll bandage it up tight to prevent any more bleeding," Evans said. "With luck, this man will heal without any complications. I couldn't feel any shattered bones in there and the bullet missed the lung."

35

"Good," Jessie said, looking into the doctor's eyes. "I'm glad that you were here—for Ki as well as for this man."

"I did nothing that any other qualified doctor couldn't have done just as well."

"I don't agree," Jessie said as the man expertly bandaged the wound.

Evans stood up and faced the giants. "This man needs to be in a hospital, not on the floor of a railroad car."

"Nate is still alive, ain't he?" Abe rumbled.

"His bandages need to be changed and that wound cleaned."

"We'll see what we can do," Eli said flatly.

Dr. Evans's cheeks burned, and he was about to say something when Jessie took his arm and and pulled him outside the coach, where they could speak in private.

"I know that you have a practice here," she said, "but I didn't get the impression that it is flourishing."

"You mean because you found me playing horseshoes?"

"That might have something to do with it."

"Well," Evans admitted, "things are a little slow right now."

"Would you consider riding this train on to Cheyenne if I paid for your ticket and also gave you a very fair payment for your services in return for taking care of Ki and Nate Lane?"

"I . . . well I suppose."

"Would three hundred dollars be agreeable?"

"Three hundred!" Evans beamed. "That would be more than acceptable."

"Good," Jessie said. "Then it is settled. I'll buy you a first class ticket and you will be paid in full when we reach Cheyenne."

"Miss Starbuck," he managed to say, "you really are more than generous."

"I am grateful," she responded. "Very, very grateful."

And then, Jessie went to buy the ticket for Dr. Evans. She knew that Sheriff Roach was not going to help, but perhaps there would be a real lawman waiting in Cheyenne. One with the courage to do what was right without fear of losing his life.

★

Chapter 6

By the time that their train rolled through northern Utah, Jessie had become well-acquainted with Dr. Evans. She learned that they were the same age and had many of the same likes and dislikes in music, food and literature.

"My father was also a doctor," Edward told her one afternoon as they were seated in the diner coach, enjoying a cup of coffee after a leisurely meal. "He was a surgeon in the Union Army. I don't think he ever quite recovered from the horror of that war."

"I suppose he saw a great deal of suffering."

"More in two years than most surgeons have in their entire lives," Edward said. "My father said the fighting was savage. He said that after a battle, there were so many wounded and so few doctors on either side that they had to resort to hacksaw surgery."

"That must have been very demoralizing to a man trained in the latest surgical techniques."

"It was," Edward said. "My father said that the wounded were stacked in the hospital tents like cords of wood. He said that there was such massive bloodshed that all he did was amputate, cauterize and stitch, then pray that the patient did not die of shock."

Jessie shook her head. "I've heard those tragic war stories, too. I hope that this country never, ever goes to war with itself again."

"Was your father in it?"

"No," Jessie said. "He was always a businessman. Long before the Civil War he founded a small import and export business in San Francisco. Pretty soon the business grew so large that he bought a warehouse and then an old wooden ship. One ship became many and my father was one of the first to convert his merchant vessels from sail to steam and then from wooden hulls to steel plated ones."

"He sounds like an innovator."

"He was. He just had a knack for making money but he never forgot that it was the common working man and woman that made his own fortune possible. My father rewarded merit, and he decried inefficiency. He also sponsored democracy and capitalism."

"He sounds like quite a man."

"He was," Jessie said. "It was his principles that were the cause of his assassination."

"Assassination?"

"Yes," Jessie said. "There was an international cartel. A group of the world's most rich and powerful who wanted my father to join their quest to form an international banking system whose founders would control the world's money supply and, therefore, it's wealth."

"Are you serious!"

"I am. My father refused and they killed him," Jessie said, mouth crimped down at the corners. "It happened right on our Texas ranch. After that, I vowed to do all I can to stamp out the corrupt and the powerful. Especially those in public office."

"You mean even down to the level of men like Sheriff Roach?"

"Exactly. A man like that should be tossed out of office, but sometimes he has either the money or the political connections to retain power."

Dr. Evans shook his head. "Forgive me for making the point, Miss Starbuck, but you have a good deal of power yourself. Isn't there some inconsistency in your values?"

"I don't think so. In the free enterprise system, an entrepreneur is judged fairly on the criteria of profit or loss."

"But profit might only be indicative of the level of exploitation used against one's own employees."

"No," Jessie said. "I pay the highest wages wherever my enterprises are located. Always the highest, and I do it because my managers are compensated for their productivity."

"I see," Edward said. "But in medicine, we don't think about such things as productivity."

"You should. Perhaps," Jessie conceded, "not in the nature of the quantity of your production, but in its quality. And I'm sure that you provide very high quality service. That's why I wanted you to join us at least as far as Cheyenne."

"I'm glad that you did for reasons besides the money, which I can most certainly use."

"Why did you come west? You seem like the sort of man who could have made a handsome living back in New England. But out here, well, I know that there are so many quacks and snake oil peddlers that folks often aren't willing to fairly compensate a real doctor."

Edward shrugged. "I always wanted to see the West. When I was a boy, Buffalo Bill's Wild West came through town and I fell in love with its romance. I *had* to come out and be a part of it."

Jessie leaned forward, chin resting on the back of her

hand. "And have you found what you expected?"

"No," he confessed. "I arrived in Reno with a letter of introduction from my father to a distant aquaintance, Dr. Cline. He took me in, gave me a place to practice medicine, but he never has really supported me or even attempted to upgrade his own techniques with newer ones that I learned at Harvard. I think he was almost relieved when I decided to accompany you to Cheyenne."

"That's unfortunate," Jessie said, "but hardly surprising. I imagine Dr. Cline has been practicing frontier medicine a long, long time and he feels a little threatened by someone with better training."

"Perhaps," Edward said. "But he shouldn't. And to not even try and upgrade his skills or read about new techniques and discoveries in medicine is something I find very difficult to understand."

"Maybe Reno isn't where you are supposed to be."

"That's what I was thinking. Perhaps you were sent as the answer to my prayers, telling me that I should try Cheyenne, or Denver."

"Or even Texas," Jessie heard herself say as their eyes met and she felt a shiver of excitement.

"Texas," he breathed, with a faraway look. "The word makes me think of the Alamo. General Santa Anna. Sam Houston and Jim Bowie. The famed Texas Rangers."

"It's a great land," she told him. "There are parts of it that are a lot like this high desert sagebrush country. There are other parts that are just rolling grassy plains, like much of eastern Wyoming. And down around the Gulf of California, it is almost tropical."

"It sounds wonderful," he said. "Do you need any personal attention, Miss Starbuck?"

She felt her cheeks warm as he looked deeply into her green eyes. "I might."

41

• • •

Cheyenne had become one of the main railroad repair and employment centers on the transcontinental railroad line. It was also the distribution point for goods flowing south to Denver and into the northern plains country, where huge cattle outfits had finally wrestled the open grazing lands from the Indian and the buffalo. The town was booming, and as their train rolled off the Big Horn Mountains into Cheyenne, Jessie was filled with new determination to intercede on the behalf of the Lane brothers.

She and Dr. Evans paid them one last visit, which obviously did not set well with Abe and Eli Hogan.

"We'll find our own damn doctor if he needs one," Abe snarled as Dr. Evans changed Nate Lane's bandage.

"The wound is healing cleanly," the doctor told his patient. "The main thing is that you cannot lift anything heavy or do anything strenuous. It is not completely healed and if the scab is torn loose before the healing process is completed, it could cause heavy bleeding and a dangerous infection."

Nate dipped his chin. "It don't much matter now, does it, Doc? Either I bleed to death, strangle at the end of a rope or get shot in the back like my brother. It all works out to about the same."

"Shut up, Nate!" Abe snapped. "You'll get your day before the judge."

"A judge that you Hogans have bought and paid for!" Nate cried. He looked to Jessie. "Ma'am, if you let them take me and my two brothers off this train and ride south, we are goners!"

"I said shut up!" Abe yelled, advancing on the man.

But Jessie moved to confront the huge deputy. Nate, like his brothers, was probably about five feet, nine inches tall and weighed less than 160 pounds soaking wet. His

42

hair was black, his eyes dark brown, and his face was rather heart-shaped. Like his brothers, Nate had delicate features, which were in sharp contrast with the brutish Hogan brothers.

"I'm going to get a marshal as soon as we arrive in Cheyenne. I'm going to make sure that nothing else goes wrong and that you and your brothers receive protection."

"Lady," Abe warned, "if you find a marshal and he wants to butt into our business, he'll regret it. We are taking these three men to trial in Santa Fe and I don't give a damn about what any marshal says."

"We'll see about that," Jessie said as she turned and left to prepare to depart the railroad. "We'll just see."

As the train neared Cheyenne, Jessie gathered her personal things and called a little meeting with Ki and the doctor. "I'm going to find the marshal before I do anything else," she told them. "Ed, if you could help Ki and get us all rooms at the Cattleman's Inn, it would be appeciated."

Ki pushed to his feet but felt very unsteady and a little light-headed. The numbness in his extremities was gone, but his toes and fingers tingled a warning, and the samurai knew that he was far from being completely recovered.

"Jessie, I need to do more than just sit in a hotel room while you do all the work."

"You will do more," Jessie promised. "I see a big improvement in you every day. Isn't that right, Doctor?"

"Absolutely. In fact, you're making remarkably good progress."

"Thanks to you," Ki said, "but I still need to help now."

"The best thing you can do now is just to rest and recover," Jessie said.

Ki knew that Jessie was right, but it was hard to accept that, for the very first time, he was the one that needed all the help.

"Ed, if you'll take my bags with you to the hotel, I'd appreciate it," Jessie said, preparing to go search for a marshal.

"Sure," he said, "but are you certain that you'll be all right?"

"Yes." Jessie removed her six-gun from its holster and placed it into her handbag. "And that's why I will not let this out of my grip."

Jessie bid the two men good-bye just as the train pulled into the Cheyenne depot. O'Brien was standing by the exit, and his old mug bore a worried expression. "You be careful out there—especially if you see them damned Hogan brothers."

"I will," Jessie promised. "However, I hardly think they are stupid enough to try and shoot me in public."

"You never know. It wouldn't bother them a whit to gun down a lady like yourself."

Jessie squeezed the conductor's arm. "Thanks for your help."

"Wish I could have done more. Hell, maybe I should have done more."

"No," Jessie said consolingly. "You're not a lawman and you have no authority. The last thing I'd have wanted was to have to tell your wife and children that I got their father shot."

O'Brien grinned and patted his stomach. "I do make a pretty big target."

"Yes you do," Jessie said, trying to sound happy despite her worry. "Good-bye."

O'Brien hugged her like a father and then Jessie leapt lightly onto the passenger platform. She turned to glance back in case Ki and the doctor were waving from the private coach. They weren't, but she did see the Hogan brothers as they bullied and prodded their frightened captives off the train and herded them toward a line of waiting carriages for hire.

Jessie hurried away. She knew that if she did not find an honest United States marshal or at least a good sheriff this time, the Hogan brothers would be on their way south before they could be stopped and questioned by the Cheyenne authorities.

Time, it seemed, was always running against her, and with Ki still recovering, she felt alone and rather helpless to stop the Hogans before they shed even more blood.

★

Chapter 7

Newly appointed Marshal Pete Melrose shined his badge with the back of his sleeve and then kissed his wife good-bye. "I'll be home for supper," he promised. "You take care of yourself and that baby!"

Julie Melrose smiled at her husband. "Doctor says it could come any day now, Pete. Says it's going to be a big one. Most likely a son."

"I'd sure like that," Pete said, still gulping down the cookies he'd had for dessert after his dinner. "See ya later!"

Julie blew him a kiss and Pete swelled up with pride. He figured he was about the luckiest man in Wyoming, to have such a young, pretty wife. He was old enough to be her father, almost, but that didn't mean anything between them. With their first child, they'd grown even closer, which had not seemed possible. And maybe someday he'd be able to buy them a nice house. Hell, he'd only been a marshal four months, and he was already doing better than he ever had at shoeing horses or, before that, tending bar.

Pete had never felt better toward the world, and as he marched up the main street of Cheyenne, he was greeted by most everyone he met. Resisting the impulse to stop and gossip, he kept a serious face and tipped his hat to them as he walked on toward his office. His predecessor, Marshal Archie Hunt, had taught him that a lawman always needed to look serious lest people take him for a joke, and he had to appear as if he were always busy, lest someone got it in their mind that they might save the city a little of its money by cutting the marshal's salary.

Pete remembered that advice, along with a lot of other things Archie had told him during the two weeks that he had been in training for this job. A frontier marshal had to carry a gun at all times and look official. He had to be friendly, but a little aloof, and he had to be damned careful about the friends he chose, because the day might come when he'd have to arrest them.

Marshal Pete Melrose had written it all down on sheets of paper that he still referred to daily. Marshal Hunt had been a very respected lawman, and he'd retired with a gold watch, just like the ones the Union Pacific gave its conductors when they left the railroad.

Cheyenne was booming. Pete figured that in another year or two he could hire a young fire-eater to be his deputy and do the unpleasant work of the lawman—patrolling the saloons at night and arresting the drunks. Or maybe breaking up domestic squabbles and fistfights, where sometimes the combatants would both turn on whoever interfered with their fun. Yep, those were the parts of being a marshal that no man enjoyed. They were better suited for a young, single lawman with ambition and dedication. Not one with a pregnant wife.

"Marshal?"

Pete looked up to see the most beautiful woman he'd ever laid eyes upon. Prettier even, he had to admit, than

47

Julie. She was tall, almost as tall as himself, and younger. Her bronze-colored hair glistened in the sunlight and her figure was . . . well, it was what Julie's had been before she had gotten with child and put on an extra twenty pounds.

"Are you Marshal Melrose?"

He realized that he was staring at her. "Why, yes, ma'am! What can I do for you?"

"We have a big problem," Jessie said, though his first impression was that a woman this beautiful couldn't possibly have a problem of any kind that fifty men wouldn't kill themselves to fix.

"A problem?"

"Yes." Quickly Jessie explained and finished by saying, "I don't know where those two so-called deputies are at the moment but it would not surprise me in the least if they were buying horses and provisions for the trail down to Santa Fe."

"Aw, now I doubt they'd just get off the train and leave town like that!" Pete snapped his fingers. He was good at it, quick and loud. He snapped them again, but the woman hardly noticed.

"We've got to find them and stop them before they can leave Cheyenne," Jessie said. "There is no telling what will happen to those Lane brothers, but I'd say they'll be shot very soon."

"But you don't know that!" Pete smiled, wanting to see her smile, but it was not to be. "Ma 'am. You seem upset over this whole thing. I think you might just be jumping to some wrong conclusions."

Jessie blinked. "Didn't you hear what I've said? Didn't you hear me say that one of the prisoners has already been shot to death and another was wounded along with my friend, Ki?"

48

"Yes, but . . . well, you admitted that no one saw the attempted escape. I got to give deputies the benefit of the doubt over a passel of murderers."

"But what if they really aren't murderers!"

He swallowed. She was beautiful, but she was going to give him a bad time, and Pete decided he'd just as soon be rid of her. "Tell you what, let me see if I can find them and I'll ask for some papers."

"And if they do not have proof either that the Lanes are wanted or that they have legal authority to apprehend them, then what?"

"Well, then I'll turn the prisoners loose!" Pete heard himself declare. "Otherwise, damn near anybody could just up and arrest anybody without any authority at all."

"Exactly!" Jessie smiled with relief. "Before we find them, could we go to your office and see if you have any Wanted posters on the Lane brothers—or on the Hogans, for that matter?"

"Why, sure!"

Pete offered the lady his arm, thinking she might be pleased to be escorted down the street on the arm of one of Cheyenne's most popular and important citizens. But she pretended she didn't see his arm, and he dropped it and let her walk alongside unattached.

When they reached the office, Pete went to his desk and removed a stack of Wanted posters. Smiling at the lady, he sat down behind his desk and quickly began to thumb through them. It took only about three or four minutes, but he was acutely aware of the woman's lovely green eyes boring into him. He could not imagine she found him anything but handsome and professional.

"Sorry," he said, when he had thumbed through the entire stack, "but no Hogan brothers."

"But no Lane brothers, either," Jessie argued.

"That's true."

"Then will you demand to see the papers authorizing their deputization and, if it is not forthcoming, insist that the prisoners be released?"

"Why, I suppose that I will," he said, not liking the way she was trying to crowd him into a corner.

"Then let's go."

Pete had been intending to brush up a little on his office cleaning chores this afternoon, and it galled him to change his schedule, especially when he was practically being ordered to do so.

"Now, ma'am, I don't—"

"Marshal Melrose," Jessie said, holding the door open, "I happen to know the governor of Wyoming and if you don't cooperate with me on this matter, he is going to hear about your lack of commitment to duty."

"Lack of commitment? Aw, come on, ma'am! All I'm sayin' is what in the heck is the big hurry! Those men aren't going to leave the minute they hit town. Like everyone else that gets off that train, they'll be tired and hungry. They'll want a drink in a saloon, a steak and a good night's sleep."

"With three prisoners chained to their wrists?" Jessie shook her head. "Not very likely, Marshal. Now are you coming—or should I telegram the governor?"

"I'm comin'! But tarnation, Miss Starbuck, you do push a man."

"I didn't ask you to accept this job. But since you have it, you owe it a certain amount of responsibility."

"I know my duties."

"Then carry them out."

Melrose couldn't seem to win a single point arguing with this woman, but then he couldn't win them with Julie, either. "All right," he said, "let's go find them and get right to the bottom of this."

"Good," Jessie said.

Pete let her walk out first. He measured the slender but definitely feminine width of her hips and admired the tiny circumference of her waist. He saw an ankle flash and he felt sexually aroused. Guilt flooded over him because of his pregnant wife, but when they stepped outside and Jessie started telling him again how bad the Hogan brothers were and how they ought to be arrested and held, his sexual arousal died.

What was immediately obvious was that this was a strong and decisive woman. One used to having her way. Pete stifled a grin. He'd bet she liked to couple with men from the top position, and damned if he wouldn't let her do it to him any old way she wanted—if he were single again.

It took them almost an hour to locate the Hogan brothers and their prisoners. By then, Jessie was very upset and Pete was ready to call off the whole thing.

"There!" Jessie cried, pointing to a buckboard that had just pulled out of a stable and was starting down the road south, toward Denver.

"Well, they're gone," he said hopefully, but Jessie went flying down the road after them.

Pete might just have let her go except that the damned woman pulled a six-gun out of her purse and opened fire. Pedestrians dove for cover. The Hogan brothers pulled iron and spun around. When they saw Jessie, they looked as if they wanted to shoot her, but instead they started cussing. It was something awful to hear, especially since it was directed to a woman.

"Now you men stop that language," Pete called, breaking into a trot and overtaking them. "I won't have a woman talked to like that in my town."

"Is that right?" Abe turned his wicked gaze from Jessie, and Pete felt a shiver pass down his spine. These were

51

the biggest, orneriest and ugliest sonsabitches he had ever seen.

"Yeah," Pete said, trying to inject a little authority into his voice but failing. "We even have an ordinance against cussin' out women in Cheyenne."

"Well you can take your ordinance and shove it up your fat ass, Marshal!"

Pete blinked and felt his legs go weak. Jessie was staring at him, and Pete knew that he had to say something in response. "I promised Miss Starbuck I'd ask you men for some kind of proof that you are either deputized, or that your prisoners are really wanted for murder down in New Mexico."

"We are deputized," Eli said, "and these three bastards will hang for the crimes they have committed."

Considering the size and ferocity of the two men, their word was good enough for Pete. He looked at Jessie, eyes begging for understanding.

"I demand that they either show you proof, or you take custody of the prisoners," Jessie said, her gun still in her fist.

Now Pete understood what it felt like to be a rat in a trap with no means of escape. He looked at the Hogan brothers as if to ask them for something, anything that would satisfy the woman.

"We cain't read," Abe said. "Piece o' paper means nothin' to us."

"Well," Pete said, seizing this as a perfectly valid explanation, "that settles it then."

"No it doesn't!" Jessie cried in anger. She raised her gun and pointed it at the brothers, who responded by pointing their own weapons back at her.

"Marshal, unless you are completely worthless, you'd better tell her to put that thing away," Eli rumbled. "What we have here is a Mexican standoff and we ain't the ones that are going to back down."

"Neither am I!" Jessie said, determined that the Hogan brothers were not going to leave with their doomed prisoners.

"Marshal, we're leavin' Cheyenne right now!" Eli called. "And if she opens fire, we'll kill her—then you!"

To emphasize their point, Abe turned his gun on Pete and cocked back the hammer. Pete felt his heart begin to bang against the insides of his ribs. He tried to swallow, but he found his mouth was as dry as sand, and he had a sudden, uncontrollable urge to urinate in his pants. He felt a rush of warm water flood down his leg and was so ashamed that an involuntary groan escaped his lips.

"Please," he managed to whisper. "I've got a wife due to have a baby! This ain't worth us all dying over, Miss Starbuck! It just ain't!"

Jessie glanced sideways at the marshal, and she could not help but notice the dark stain on his light brown pantleg. Only then did she realize that he was terrified and that he was also right. This was not the time and the place to force a showdown. Later, maybe. Later, when she had the samurai or at least the element of surprise on her side. But not now.

"All right," she managed to whisper as she lowered her pistol and turned her back on the buckboard. "All right!"

The Hogan brothers guffawed like a pair of braying mules, and one of the Lane brothers begged for help but was silenced by the back of Eli's hand.

Jessie kept walking. She didn't want to see the triumphant look on the faces of the Hogan brothers, and neither did she want ever to look at the marshal again.

Behind her, turning his head back and forth from a retreating Jessie to the vanishing buckboard, Marshal Pete

Melrose stood exposed and shamed before all the towns-folk. He heard snickers and then cruel laughter from a cluster of men standing outside the Horseshoe Club, and he wished that he were dead.

"Hey, Marshal Pants Pisser!" a man called, and that set them all whooping with laughter.

The laughter grew so loud in his ears that Pete covered them, but when the sound would not die, he hurried away, tearing his badge from his coat and hurling it at the dirt. He passed on up the street, running now, going to the comfort of Julie's arms. They would pull stakes this very day. Put the humiliation of his cowardice behind and go somewhere far enough away that he would never again hear himself called a Pants Pisser.

But even as Pete ran up the street, people watching him with contempt-filled eyes, he knew that he would never again be a proud man. And never again would he be considered a man of high and respected standing in his community.

God damn you, Archie Hunter! he raged from within. You never told me what to do if this happened!

★

Chapter 8

That night, after dinner in her room, Jessie confessed to Edward that she was sure she had failed and that the Lane brothers were already as good as dead.

"That doesn't necessarily have to be the case," Edward said, twirling the amber liquid in his brandy glass. "It doesn't have to be the case at all."

Jessie took a sip of her own brandy. The room felt warm, and so she walked over to her window and opened it a little to admit some fresh air. "What do you mean?" she asked, turning around to face the doctor.

"I mean that if I came along to take care of the samurai's medical needs a while longer, we could go after those men. Who knows? Perhaps we can finally exact some justice in Denver. And besides, you are traveling that way anyhow."

"Would it be all right for Ki to travel in his present condition?"

"Most certainly!" Dr. Evans smiled. "Provided, of course, that he has proper medical supervision."

"Of course," Jessie said. "And of course, you would be well paid for your services."

Edward placed his glass down and came over to stand beside Jessie. "Money," he said, running his hand lightly up her arm, "isn't payment enough, Jessie. I was thinking that there is something that I'd treasure much more than cash."

She smiled, shivered a little at his touch and slipped her hand around his waist. "What on earth could you mean?" she asked in a teasing way.

"I mean that I've wanted you from the moment I first saw you. I mean that you are driving me crazy with desire. I mean that I want to make love to you starting right now."

When their lips met, Jessie felt a tremble of desire. She pressed her body to his, and the heat between them made her pulse beat faster. Her questing tongue pushed its way into his mouth, and she heard him groan. Without breaking their kiss, they stumbled over to the bed, hands tearing off clothes, bodies already starting to push and throb.

"Hurry!" she whispered as she tore off the last of her undergarments and stood before him. "I've wanted you too."

He laughed in his throat and removed the last stitches of his clothing. His hand, with its fine, gentle touch, cupped her lush breast, and his lips were hot on her hard nipples. Jessie sighed. She arched her back as the doctor's tongue began to trace wet circles around her nipples. Her hand stroked his hairy chest and then it slipped down between his legs. She did not hold him at first, but let her fingers brush gently up and down his long, hard shaft.

He stepped back from her for a moment, and his eyes were glazed with desire as he drank in her beauty. "You are one of the most beautiful women I've ever seen," he said in a voice hoarse with desire.

Jessie smiled and cupped his sack, and she felt him tremble. She moved close again, rubbing his shaft between her legs until she grew wet, and then she slipped him just inside her body.

"Don't move," she whispered.

"Impossible," he moaned, hips already starting to jerk as he sought to impale her with his thick manhood.

Jessie fell back on her bed, parting her lovely legs for his entry. For a moment, he stood poised, taut and frozen, his breathing already fast. Then, she took his shaft in her hands and guided it into her moist, quivering womanhood.

Jessie gasped as Edward plunged deep inside of her, and then she sighed with contentment as the man at last had his way with her body. He stood bent over her, hands gripping her hips as he began to thrust. At first, his thrusts were controlled and so a little clumsy as he attempted to be gentle. Jessie appreciated his concern, but when she wrapped her legs around his hips and began to milk him powerfully, he abandoned all control and fell upon her like a famished animal.

"Easy, my darling," she panted as he drove himself at her in a frenzy of passion. "Make it last a few lovely moments."

With great difficulty, he slowed his hard thrusting, and Jessie began to milk him expertly. He groaned and shivered. "I never had a woman that compares to you, Jessie. What are you doing to me!"

"I'm doing what women were meant to do to men," she said, her hips pumping harder and harder as she felt herself lifting quickly toward her own orgasm.

Edward's mouth covered her own, and he became a wild thing in her, his manhood whipping her own passion higher and higher until she could no longer control her body.

"Yes!" she cried, her head rolling from side to side and her buttocks thrusting furiously at him. "Yes!"

His body convulsed, and she felt his flooding seed fill her insides as her own body began to spasm and her fingernails bit deep into the flesh of his buttocks. Their cries of pleasure filled the room, and their bodies stiffened and then went limp.

"Dear woman!" he whispered passionately. "You have ruined me for anyone else."

Jessie waited a moment, until she could catch her breath. She hugged him tightly and said, "No I haven't."

"But compared to the others I've had—"

She silenced his words with her mouth, and when she finished kissing him, she said, "Let's just talk about tonight and not think about what must be done tomorrow."

"I want you a hundred times before dawn," he said with a grin. "But I'm not man enough for that."

"How about five, or even ten?"

"Are you serious?" He stared at her.

"I am a very generous woman," she told him, rolling on top and pulling his face down between her lush breasts. "And besides, I demand a good deal of lovemaking. It relaxes me."

"Well," he said, "in that case, you are going be the most relaxed woman in Wyoming come daybreak."

Jessie laughed and spread her legs. "It's yours tonight," she whispered, "all that you could ever want."

Her words brought new life to his manhood, and soon, very soon, Jessie was moving up and down on his slick rod, her eyes glazing with her own desire.

In the morning, Jessie and Dr. Evans were tired and *very* relaxed. They had breakfast and then made preparations for leaving and going south to Denver. Jessie bought a very serviceable coach and a team of fine horses. Since the doctor was not skilled at driving and Ki was still too injured, she drove out of Cheyenne herself.

"With luck," she told her companions, "we can overtake them in Denver."

"But what if we don't," Edward asked. "I mean, they have almost a full day's head start on us."

"In that case, we will go right on down to Santa Fe."

"I am feeling much better every day," Ki said. "And this fresh air will hasten my recovery."

"Of course it will," Dr. Evans said. "Nothing like good fresh air to restore a man to health."

Jessie smiled. A few miles south of Cheyenne they saw a big herd of antelope grazing on the same hills where only a few years ago buffalo had grazed.

"Have you ever been to Denver?" Jessie asked the doctor.

"No. Is it bigger than Cheyenne?"

"Smaller," Jessie said. "But the town fathers are trying to raise enough money to build a rail line up to Cheyenne. If they can do that, I think that Denver may one day rival and even exceed the size and importance of Cheyenne."

"What about Santa Fe?" the doctor asked. "I can hardly wait to see it. I've heard and read the stories about that old frontier town."

"It is rich with history," Jessie agreed. "Even the earliest Spaniards came there to trade. But I'm still hoping that we can rescue the Lane brothers before then."

"It would be nice," Dr. Evans said, "but we sure haven't had much luck with the local law officials so far."

"We've been very unlucky," Jessie agreed. "You never know what you will find in these towns. Some sheriffs and marshals are the finest men you'd ever want to meet. Others . . . well, you've seen their kind and it is regrettable."

Jessie drove along in silence for a few more minutes. Despite having not gotten any sleep the night before, she felt very good. Lovemaking did relax her and the fresh air of Wyoming was bracing. She loved these rolling, grassy hills.

"We can't give up now," she said, more to herself than to them. "We just have to do whatever we can to see that justice is done and that the Hogan brothers aren't allowed to get away with any more murder."

Ki nodded. He would do whatever she wanted, and from the rather dazed expression on Dr. Evans's young face, Ki suspected that the doctor would follow Jessie to hell and back if asked.

★

Chapter 9

The air was warm and balmy that afternoon as they traveled along the very well-worn road to Denver. Ki rested comfortably in the coach, and the team that Jessie drove was so well behaved that they were a pleasure to handle. They passed many others along the way—freighters, cowboys riding in search of a job or a good time, ranchers and even a few old Conestoga wagons loaded down with families bound both north and south.

"If there's one thing that never ceases to amaze me," Jessie said, "it's that everyone is so rootless in the West. It seems that people are constantly pulling stakes and taking off in search of a better farm, ranch or opportunity. In Europe, people are much more settled. They put down roots and they stay, sometimes on the same land one generation after the next. In Europe, to journey a hundred miles is a big thing. Out West . . . well, everyone is constantly on the move."

"As you seem to be," Edward said. "I get the feeling that even Texas isn't big enough to hold you and Ki for very long."

"Oh, but it is!" she protested. "It's just that I have businesses all over the world."

"But you also like to travel, isn't that right?"

"Yes," she admitted. "Especially in the West. Ki and I both love the adventure."

The young doctor frowned. "He is a very interesting man, your Ki. Tell me about him."

"His father was an American sea captain and his mother was a beautiful Japanese woman of the highest social class. They fell in love and then Ki's father took ill and died."

"And his mother brought him to America?"

"No," Jessie said. "His mother was ostracized for having married an American. You see, the Japanese consider all other races to be inferior."

"Humph," Edward snorted. "And so the poor woman was cast out by her own family?"

"Yes. She was able to support herself and her half-breed child for a few years, but her delicate constitution failed and Ki became an orphan. He had a terrible childhood. He almost died of starvation."

"They would allow that to happen?"

"Yes," Jessie said. "The Japanese are very rigid in their attitudes. Any man or woman who marries one of another race as much as forfeits their rights in that ancient country. Ki does not like to talk about the years he barely managed to survive as a street thief and a beggar."

"Did he finally just grow up and somehow manage to gain passage on a ship to America?"

"He was saved by a *ronin*," Jessie said.

"A what?"

"*Ronin*," Jessie repeated. "In Japanese, that means a 'wave man.' It comes from the observation that waves on the sea are aimless, moving without purpose. A *ronin*

62

is a samurai who has lost his master. And without a master, a samurai has no purpose."

"Then what happens to them?"

"They search for another master to serve. And if they cannot find one, they just exist until it is time for them to die."

Jessie knew this was difficult for Edward to digest. The idea that someone was living to serve another was almost impossible for an independent-minded American to accept, yet this was exactly how the Japanese thought and lived.

"The *ronin* who saved Ki was named Hirata," Jessie continued after a few moments. "He took pity on Ki. He took him off the street and gave him a home and a mission—to become a samurai. Hirata taught Ki everything about being samurai. From their noble code of honor to their secret rituals and ways of fighting. He taught Ki the art of *te* or hand fighting. He spent the last years of his life teaching Ki to become *ninja*, the most feared and disciplined of all the samurai."

"*Ninja?*"

"Yes," Jessie said. "They are the invisible assassins of Japan. They spend years learning to stalk a target without being observed and then to kill it. If they fail their mission, they are expected to impale themselves on their swords."

"And they do this?" Edward asked, looking appalled.

"Yes," Jessie replied. "In fact, when Hirata was satisfied that he could teach Ki no more, he ended his own life that ancient and honorable way. One or two deep slashes with his sword through the stomach."

The young doctor shook his head in amazement and revulsion. "I don't think that I would like to visit Japan if they condone suicide," he said. "In the mind of a physican devoted to healing, the act of taking one's own life is inexcusable."

"I can understand that," Jessie said. "Yet, in many societies, the old or the sick are either abandoned or expected to end their lives for the benefit of their society."

Dr. Evans was silent for a while as he digested that bit of information. Finally, he asked a question that was hard on his mind. "Do you and Ki ever think about . . . well, you know."

"Making love?"

"It must be a temptation."

"It is, at times," Jessie admitted. "But no, we are close friends and excellent traveling companions. Ki is my protector and he is a wonderful person to be able to rely on when there is trouble."

"I have never met anyone even remotely like him," the doctor said.

"Tell me more about your background," Jessie said.

"Not much else to tell. I had a happy childhood and was born to privileges. Being the only son, it disappointed my father very much when I decided to go west in search of adventure and a new way of life. My father had been planning to give me his practice. I would have quickly become a rather well-to-do man."

"But you threw it all away."

Edward chuckled. "It sounds crazy, doesn't it? Working only half-time in Reno, accepting chickens, cows and even tools in lieu of cash for services was a real eye-opener for me. Of course, I never wrote and told my parents that I was living in a flophouse and barely able to feed and clothe myself as a frontier doctor."

"It's to your credit that you didn't give up and go back to your parents and their easy, comfortable way of life."

"I've always been stubborn," Edward told her. "And besides, I saw it as a choice between staying in the West and dealing with really serious injuries such as knife and bullet wounds, or returning to the East and treating the often petty but highly remunerative afflictions of the wealthy."

"I'm glad that you decided to stay," Jessie said. "I think that, more and more, we will see good, professional doctors coming to the West and replacing the tooth-pullers and charlatans that have dominated frontier medicine."

"As long as we can survive," Edward said, "we'll come and stay. I know that I would find it very tame going back East now that the Civil War is long since past."

Jessie and Edward chatted all afternoon, but Jessie did not allow the team to dawdle. She pushed them hard because it was her intention to overtake the Hogan brothers if possible and, if not, at least to catch them in Denver. On the second day of their journey, just after daybreak, when they had gotten started, they spotted a smoking wagon off in the distance.

"What do you think?" Edward asked, squinting hard. "Do you think there is anyone there in trouble?"

"I don't know," Jessie said, hesitant to go investigate because the detour would cost them at least an hour.

"Look!" Edward cried. "Did you see that?"

"What?"

"There! A hand. It looks as if it's rising up from the bed of that burning wagon."

"That's impossible."

"I think we'd better go investigate none the less."

Jessie agreed because she could also see the hand now. It was not coming from the wagon, however, but instead appeared to belong to someone that was lying in a depression just in front of the burning wagon.

Jessie swung the team out of the rutted track leading down to Denver and cracked the lines on the rumps of her horses. Their coach rumbled forward as the two horses assumed a brisk trot. Even as they approached, the flames

65

seemed to grow higher, and by the time that they were near enough to smell the smoke, the wagon was completely engulfed by the inferno. It was then that they also saw the bodies.

There was a man, an older boy and a woman lying shot in a low spot on the prairie. About twenty feet away from them was a half-naked young woman covered with blood. She was lying on her stomach, wailing as if her heart would break.

Jessie dropped to her knees beside the young woman, covering her with a blanket that she had grabbed out of the coach. At Jessie's touch, the young woman wailed even louder, and when Jessie tried to roll her over to examine the cause of her bleeding, the woman lashed blindly at her.

"Easy," Jessie said. "We're going to help you! Please, don't be afraid!"

The woman stared up at Jessie with wild, half-crazed eyes, and for a moment, Jessie thought that she had gone mad. She could also see that the woman had been raped and stabbed once in the side.

Dr. Evans tore open his medical kit and covered her wound with bandages. "How long have you been bleeding?" he asked calmly. "Are you having trouble breathing?"

The young woman closed her eyes, and now she grabbed Jessie and hugged her very tight. At the same time she began to sob hysterically, and Jessie held her close, talking softly to her without caring if she made any sense.

"It's a nasty wound and she's lost a good deal of blood," Edward said, "but I don't think that her life is in any real danger. I could be wrong, however, if some vital organ has been damaged."

"And there is no way to tell?"

Dr. Evans checked the woman's pulse. "Her heart is beating strong and regular; her color is bad, but it's on account of the blood she's lost. If I can stave off an infection, I think she will be fine."

Jessie nodded, still holding the girl. And though she did not come right out and say it, her major worry centered on the woman's mental health. One look from her eyes conveyed a sense of terror.

"Maybe we can find out who the animals were that did this," Jessie said in a grim voice.

She looked up to see the samurai standing close. She said, "I'm afraid that you can't do anything to help this time."

But Ki was not listening, as he began to move slowly, painfully, around the area, reading tracks.

"What can he possibly learn?" Edward asked when he had finished rebandaging the girl's side.

"He can learn more than you'd think," Jessie said, watching her samurai bend over the faint indentation of a man's footprint.

"I don't suppose we can bury these poor people without a shovel," Edward said, "and we certainly can't leave them here for the coyotes and wolves. So what are we going to do?"

Jessie frowned. Edward was right. The bodies did pose a real problem. "We'll either have to load them into our coach and wait to bury them when we find a shovel, or else I can unharness one of our horses, ride back to the main track and wait until someone passes with a shovel."

Ki stood upright and looked at Jessie. "This is not a good country for a woman alone. I think we should load the bodies and put the girl and myself on top of the coach."

"I agree," Edward said quickly. "It would be much faster that way."

"All right," Jessie said. "Ki, would you come and stay with this young lady while I help Edward load the bodies?"

"I am able to do that," Ki said stubbornly.

Within a half hour, the three bodies had all been wrapped and placed inside the coach. Jessie and Edward helped the young woman up onto the roof of the coach, and Ki followed. The girl had not spoken a single word thus far, and now she seemed to have withdrawn into herself and would not acknowledge their questions.

"She'll be all right in time," Jessie said. She looked to her doctor. "Won't she?"

"I'm a general practitioner and surgeon," Edward replied, "not a psychiatrist. I can't answer your question, Jessie. The girl is obviously in a state of complete shock. Usually, time will heal, but not always."

Jessie took one last look at the wagon as the flames caused it to buckle and collapse in a shower of embers and ash. "I can't imagine the kind of men that would do this to a family."

"I can," the samurai said from behind her. "The Hogans."

Jessie twisted around. "You don't think—"

"I don't know," Ki interrupted, "but it's a possibility. They are also traveling this way."

"But the fire! It couldn't have been set more than a half hour before we arrived."

"I know," the samurai said, "and maybe the Hogans aren't as far ahead as we thought."

"If it is them, and if that young woman can identify them, then we will make sure they are put behind bars!"

Ki looked sideways into the vacant eyes of the woman who sat cross-legged on the coach with the blanket wrapped around her violated body.

"I don't think that we can count on her help," the samurai said.

Jessie understood. The young woman might not come out of her state of shock for days or even weeks—if ever. The

Hogans, in the meantime, would keep moving south, toward Santa Fe.

As her mind leapt foward, Jessie wondered if a single one of the Lane brothers was still alive.

★

Chapter 10

Nate Lane lay in the back of the high-sided wagon, shackled wrist and ankle to his two younger brothers—both beaten into unconsciousness. Their faces were covered with blood, and Orin's nose was obviously broken. Jeb was the youngest, and his cheek had been laid wide open with the barrel of Eli's six-gun.

At least, Nate thought, we are still alive.

Nate's shoulder was paining him something awful, and he knew that the bullet wound was infected. He could feel the poison from that wound seeping throughout the entire length of his body. It was going to kill him unless he was able to get medical attention before much longer.

But seeing a doctor was not among the things the Hogan brothers had planned for after their arrival in Denver. Nate had heard the pair talk about how they intended to do some drinking and carousing, maybe play a little poker and consort with some prostitutes before continuing on to Santa Fe.

Nate stared up at the sky. He and his brothers had been warned that if they ever made a sound or in any way let passersby know that they were inside this wagon, they'd be shot and so would the passersby.

The Hogan brothers had carried out their promise. Even now, when Nate recalled what had happened to that family and . . . and the young woman who had been brutally violated, his eyes filled with stinging tears and his heart beat so fast with hatred that he thought it must surely explode. Nate squeezed his eyes shut, and the memory of that terrible encounter returned as vividly as it had occurred in real life. In fact, he could even smell the gunsmoke and hear the young woman's screams.

"There's a wagon just over yonder," Abe said, "looks like it might have a broken axle."

"It's a family and they're all alone."

"Probably figured the grass was a little better a mile or two off this track for their livestock," Abe guessed. "Now, they're in a fix."

"Maybe we should pay them a little visit. Could be they'd show their gratitude if we was to help."

Abe chuckled, turned the wagon off the Denver road and drove out toward the wagon. As they drew nearer, Eli exclaimed, "Would you look at that pretty gal with the yeller hair! How old you think she is?"

There was a long pause, and then Abe chuckled. "Old enough, I reckon."

"Do you figure that's her husband, along with that older couple?"

"Husband or brother, what's the difference?" Abe spat tobacco. "You thinkin' what I'm thinkin'?"

"I get her first," Eli said.

"The hell you do!"

"We'll flip for her."

"Fair enough."

71

The two brothers flipped a coin and Eli laughed. "I win!"

"I'll give you five dollars you let me have her first," Abe said.

"Nope."

"Ya son of a bitch," Abe growled. "You always was the lucky one." When they drew up to the wagon, the older man and woman came forward. Abe and Eli could see that they were worried, and their team of horses were picketed off a little ways.

"Got a problem?" Eli asked.

"Sure do," the older man said. "I guess you can tell mighty quick that we busted an axle. You men got any tools or somethin' that would help us get on to Denver? If we could get that far, we'd sure be grateful."

"Nice family you got," Abe said, looking past the worried couple.

The older man nodded. "That there is my son-in-law, Art Spicer and my daughter Nancy."

Abe and Eli stared at Nancy. Eli said, "You sure are a pretty one. How old you be?"

The girl blushed. Her young husband's face also grew red. "That ain't a proper question for a stranger to ask."

"We ain't proper gentlemen," Abe said.

The older man and woman shifted uncomfortably. The man said, "Well, I tell you what, we thank you for checkin' up on us but we'll just get along fine. I reckon someone is bound to come along that can help."

Abe wasn't listening. "You carry any whiskey?"

"Why . . . no!"

"You wouldn't lie to me, would you?" Abe asked with a grin.

"Well . . . we have a little, but. . . ."

"You got any money?"

For a long beat, the question hung between them all. The older man was too stunned to answer, but his son-in-law shouted, "These men didn't come to help us, they came—"

It was then that Orin and Jeb surged up from the bed of the wagon to shout a warning. Nate had tried to hold them down but failed.

"Look out! They're killers!" Orin cried.

Everything had happened very fast. There were screams and gunshots, smoke and death. Nate and his brothers, certain that they would also be slaughtered, dropped to the floor of the wagon and waited for a bullet.

The bullet never came. Instead, the Hogan brothers jumped from the wagon and went hollering and yelling as they chased the screaming girl to the ground. Nate jumped to his feet and saw what the Hogan brothers did to the poor girl, how they'd stripped and violated her right out in the open.

"Stop it! Stop it!" he cried over and over.

Abe turned and emptied his gun at the wagon. The slugs ripped through the thin sideboards, but, miraculously, neither Nate nor his brothers were hit. So they hugged the floor of the wagon, listening to the weakening cries of the young woman. She went on for more than an hour, and then there was a terrible, ominous silence.

The back of the wagon bed dropped, and Nate looked up to see the Hogan brothers climbing aboard, their faces flushed from their exertions with the young woman, who Nate was sure had been murdered when they were through with her.

"It was them two," Abe hissed.

Orin and Jeb looked up and began to beg for their lives. The Hogan brothers landed on their chests and beat them half to death. Beat them so savagely that their features were

73

barely recognizable. Nate, the oldest, pulled his knees to his chest and sobbed like a helpless baby while his brothers cried and begged until they lost consciousness.

"You was warned!" Eli shouted, coming to his feet and kicking Nate in the side. "You was warned that if you made a sound, you'd pay the price. Well goddammit, you just paid!"

Nate did not said a word. He just lay there, wrapped in pain and shame until the brothers jumped down from the wagon and lifted the tailgate. Only when the wagon lurched forward, back toward the Denver road, did Nate dare to peer through the cracks in the side boards. It took him a couple minutes before he was able to see the three dead people. But worst of all was the sight of the girl with the yellow hair.

She was lying like a broken doll. All white and spread out on the grass. He caught a glimpse of bright crimson on her, and then the wagon turned and she was lost to his sight. It was right then that Nate vowed he would try to live no matter what, so that he could kill the Hogan brothers. Kill them for John, the oldest of his brothers, who'd been shot on the Central Pacific train as he'd tried to escape into the Sierras. Kill the Hogans for ambushing others of his family outside of Santa Fe and then, finally, for killing these poor, innocent travelers.

Nate looked at the bloody faces of his younger brothers, and a bounce of the wagon sent a jolt of pain through his wounded shoulder. He would need medical attention in Denver. Otherwise, he wouldn't last another three days and his vow to kill the Hogans was as worthless as spit.

"That first time, she was too damn wiggly," Eli complained as they neared the outskirts of Denver. "I couldn't hardly do her she was so wiggly."

74

Abe said, "We should have taken more time to search that busted wagon. All we got was a quart of whiskey and six dollars. They musta had more than that. Probably hidden but if we'd have spent more time, we'd have found it. Maybe hidden under the floorboards."

"Maybe," Eli said, "but what is done is done. We got a couple good pistols and rifles."

"Hell, they're just percussion! Ain't going to bring us more than twenty dollars for the lot of them in Denver."

"Twenty dollars will pay for our pleasures."

"I'm still tryin' to figure out what we're going to do with them in back," Abe growled. "Can't let 'em get away while we're doin' the town."

"Wish we could just kill the lot of 'em."

"Well, we can't!" Abe growled. "You and I both know we can't, so there's no damn sense in talkin' about it."

"We killed John. We could kill all but one and it'd be fine with Zebulon. He wouldn't be too mad."

"Don't count on it," Abe said, thinking of their father's terrible temper. "I reckon we need all three that's left if we're to get their land. Leastways, that's what's been told to us."

"Aw hell," Eli said with disgust. "If we kill 'em down to the last man, whose to stop us from just takin' their land?"

"The law," Abe said. "If word got out what we done, there'd be law comin' from all over the goddamn West to stop us. We get 'em to sign it over legal like, there ain't a damn thing that anyone can say or do once the ink is on the paper. That's what Pa keeps sayin'."

"I suppose," Eli said, "but it's a real trial. Me, I just wanted to shoot them all when we caught the bastards in California. We done that, we'd be rid of all this trouble and ridin' easy instead of bustin' our spines on this damn wagon."

75

"We're gettin' it done the way Pa told us," Abe said. "We're doin' it the right instead of the easy way. Besides, it ain't all been work. That was pure pleasure back yonder with the girl, huh?"

Eli giggled. "Sure was! I just wish she had stopped screamin' in my face and bein' so wiggly."

"Hell," Abe grunted, "I made her stop wigglin'!"

The two men laughed and laughed, while Nate stared up at big white clouds that looked so peaceful a man would think all was just right with the world, instead of so terribly wrong.

"We still ain't figured out what to do with 'em," Abe said after a while.

"I still think we should just kill 'em and be done with it."

"That's what you always think," Abe said. "Hell, you may have beat two of them to death anyway!"

"You helped!"

There was a long pause, and then Abe, sounding a little contrite, replied, "Yeah, well, the girl got my blood up and I lost my head."

Eli chuckled. "Good to see it happen to you once in a while instead of me. You want to split the twenty dollars now, or when we get to Denver Town?"

"Let's figure out what we kin do with them damn brothers first. Then we'll talk about the pleasurin' we kin do with our money."

Nate listened carefully but to no avail. After a few halfhearted suggestions, the Hogan brothers started talking and joking again about what they'd done to the yellow-haired girl back on the prairie.

Through his pain and the poison spreading from his shoulder through his body, Nate dreamed of vengeance and then the sweet mercy of his own death.

★

Chapter 11

"There she is, Denver Town," Abe growled, "and we still ain't figured out what the hell we're supposed to do with 'em."

"Slit their throats now," Eli urged. "That's what we oughta do."

"Shut up," Abe said without any heat. "We been over this one already."

"But we ain't come up with anything."

"I say we need to find ourselves a cabin or somethin' just outside of town. Bound to be one that's vacant or that we can persuade someone to let us use for awhile."

"And then what?" Eli protested. "We can't just leave 'em!"

"Sure we can. We got 'em trussed up like pigs on a platter. They're in bad shape and we can gag the bastards. Hell, Eli, all we're askin' for is just one damn night on the town. We ought to be able to fix 'em up so's we can get that much."

Eli nodded. He looked back over his shoulder. "I think

77

Nate is dyin'," he said. "That there shoulder looks kinda green and it's startin' to smell."

"You're right," Abe said. "We may have to shoot him again and bury him. Might be we ought to try and remember to buy a shovel."

"The hell with diggin'. We'll just roll him off into a draw and let the coyotes pick his bones if he can't make it down to Santa Fe."

Nate listened to all this with barely concealed terror gripping his heart. His mind feverishly worked to consider the prospects. He knew that if he did not soon get medical attention, he was a dead man. Nate was equally certain that his two younger brothers, still only half-conscious hours after their terrible beating, would be dead after being forced to sign over their New Mexico ranch lands.

"There's a place that looks empty," Abe said, turning the horses off the road and driving the wagon down a set of bumpy ruts.

The wagon stopped. Nate peeked through the cracks in the side boards and saw a dilapidated shack whose roof had partially collapsed. The boards were sun-blistered gray, but they appeared to be solid. The shack was off by itself, probably a good mile or two north of Denver.

He saw Eli jump down and step up to the door, which hung ajar on one good hinge. Eli pushed the door open and disappeared inside. He reemerged less than a minute later.

"Reckon it'll do," he said to his brother. "Ain't nothing inside worth anything. Just rat shit and rusty bean cans."

Abe tied the lines to his brake and hopped down. He walked around to the back of the wagon, and when he started to drop it, Nate closed his eyes and pretended to be either asleep or unconscious like his brothers.

"Come on out of there!" Abe ordered.

None of them moved.

"I said come on out, damn you!"

Nate heard Orin cry out in confused pain, and this was followed by the sound of his body striking the ground. Jeb was dragged out and dumped on the ground, and Nate was right on his brother's heels.

"They're all half-dead," Abe grunted as he and his big brother dragged their bodies inside the shack.

"Let's make damn sure they can't get loose," Eli said, checking the handcuffs and the chains that bound them together.

"Hell, they're set," Abe growled. "Let's close the door and git out of here. I'm thirsty!"

Nate kept his eyes screwed shut tight until he heard the creak of the door; then he rolled into a sitting position. He had worked at the handcuffs behind his back until his wrists were bloody and swollen, but now he worked at them again.

When he heard the wagon leaving, Nate cried, "Hey, Orin! Jeb! They're gone! We got to get outa here before they come back or we're finished!"

When neither one of his younger brothers roused to his call, Nate scooted over to Jeb. He kicked him a few times, until Jeb grunted, and then he backed up to him and pinched him a couple of times on his poor puffy cheeks.

"Jeb, damn you! We've got to pull together now! This is our last chance to get away!"

Jeb opened his eyes but seemed to have trouble focusing. "Huh?" he mumbled. "Don't hit me no more! Please, don't hit me no more!"

"Jeb, it's me! Nate! They've left us alone and now we gotta get out of here!"

Jeb roused a little more. He blinked and tried to focus. "Nate?"

"Yeah! It's me, your brother! Can you stand up!"

"Uh-uh," Jeb said drowsily. "Wanna go to sleep, Nate. Just leave me alone."

"Goddammit, I can't! They're coming back and they'll kill us. I got to get to a doctor!"

When Jeb's chin sagged to his chest, Nate kicked his brother again. Jeb yelped with pain.

"Jeb, you *got* to help me!"

Jeb finally seemed to understand, and together they tried to awaken Orin. It took almost an entire hour to get Orin to come awake. He was in worse shape than Nate had supposed.

"Listen," Nate said, "unless we can find a file or somethin' to break these chains, we're gonna have to all go out together. I don't know how long we got. The Hogans have already been gone a couple of hours. They could decide to come back most any time!"

"If they catch us outside, they'll kill us all for sure!" Orin whined. "I ain't gonna try to get away, Nate! They need us down in Santa Fe or else we'd already be dead."

"Listen to me!" Nate cried. "I *am* already dead if I don't get to a doctor soon! I got a shoulder that's on fire."

Jeb tried to rise to his feet but couldn't. "I ain't got no strength in me," he sobbed. "I ain't got the strength of a damned baby!"

"Sure you do!" Nate cried. "Here, if we all stand at once, we can do it! We can go through that door and hop right on down to Denver. It ain't very far. Ain't no more than a mile or two and somebody is sure to see us. Someone will help."

Jeb and Orin exchanged glances. They weren't sure they believed, but they knew that they had to try. Nate was their leader now. He was the one that had to think straight for them all.

"Come on," Nate urged, trying to stand himself and doing it but only after several futile attempts. "Come on! Take my hand, Orin. Just come up easy."

Orin moaned and they struggled until he was on his feet.

"Jeb?"

"I can't," he whispered. "I hurt so bad, Nate. I feel like I'm goin' to die!"

"You *will* die if we don't get out of here before they get back!"

Jeb looked up at them and pleaded with his eyes to be left alone.

"Get up!" Nate commanded. "Damn you, get on your feet!"

Jeb whimpered as he tried to rise. He would not have made it if his older brothers hadn't dragged him erect.

For a moment, they all swayed in a fading light as a growing sense of hoplessness spread over them. Finally, Orin said, "Nate, with our ankles all bound up, how we gonna do this!"

"We've got to hop," he said. "I been thinking about it. Hopping is the only way and we got to do it all together."

They looked at him as if he were insane. It made Nate cry, "We got no choice!"

He lowered his voice. "All right. Let's line up to face the door and we'll hop to it. Once outside, maybe we'll be seen right away by someone passin' by. Maybe our luck is finally about to change."

A faint glimmer of hope touched their disfigured features. "All right," Nate breathed, "on three, we hop. One, two . . . three!"

They all hopped, but it didn't amount to anything. Jeb barely moved and he lost his balance, then pitched forward, striking Orin. They both went down, and Orin cried out as the shackle on his ankle twisted deep into his flesh. Nate barely managed to stay erect.

"Okay," he whispered, "I was wrong. We ain't goin' nowhere by hoppin'. Jeb ain't got the strength for it."

"And neither do I," Orin said, his voice choking with pain. "I don't think this is gonna work, Nate! I think we just better stay here and wait for them. They *need* us to sign some kind of papers."

"That's right," Nate said, "they do! But after that, they'll kill us and we won't have any help. But if we could get away here in Denver, we could find someone who might hide us—or get the law."

"The law won't stand up to the likes of the Hogans!" Orin cried. "You seen what the law did in Reno and Cheyenne!"

Nate cursed and threw his head around in a fit of anger and frustration. "Well, just what are we supposed to do then, give up? I'm not ready to die! Not until I take them bastards with me!"

Silence stretched between them. They were all breathing hard, as if they were winded from running a long ways, only it was really because they were scared half-witless.

"I can't do it," Jeb said and choked. "I got no strength to go anyplace, Nate, I swear that I don't."

Nate believed his youngest brother. A small sob escaped from his mouth, and he bit his lower lip to keep it from happening a second time. He could taste his own blood.

"Maybe they'll get themselves killed in Denver," Orin said hopefully. "Maybe they'll just get shot!"

Nate shook his head. "I can't count on that," he said. "I can't count on it at all."

Darkness was claiming the inside of the cabin. When they'd been thrown in here, it had been light enough to see things; now, it was almost dark.

"What are you doin', Nate?" Orin asked. "Nate, stop movin' around! You're hurtin my ankles and wrists when you move that way!"

"Damn your ankles and wrists!" Nate cried. "I'm looking for something. Anything that will help me get loose of these handcuffs and shackles!"

"Ain't nothin' gonna set you free but the key in their pocket," Jeb gasped. "Ain't nothin' else can do it."

Nate stopped struggling and dragged his fingers hopelessly through the dirt and debris on the floor. He stared at his brothers and felt hot tears roll down his cheeks.

"Ain't no key gonna set me loose," he breathed, "it's gonna be death that'll do it. Dyin' is all. That's the only way I'm going to be free now."

Orin and Jeb looked strangely at him, but Nate didn't notice. He lay back down on the floor and let the hot tide of his fever sweep away everything, including his pain.

Nate awoke to the cries of his brothers, and then he felt rough hands lifting and pulling him back outside. A few moments later, he realized he was back in the wagon bed and they were again on the move.

"Hell of a time!" Abe laughed. "Damned if I didn't want to bring that little redheaded woman along with us to Santa Fe! She was ready!"

"Then why didn't ya!"

There was a long silence, and than Abe said, "And what was I supposed to say about them three in the back we got shackled and chained?"

"You could have told her they were all dead men that wanted to be tied and buried together."

"Huh?"

Eli burst into raw laughter. "Hell, you could tell her that

83

we are bound for Santa Fe and we got a notion to feed buzzards on the way!"

Abe burst into guffaws along with his brother. And behind them, Nate felt the flames of hell lick his feet.

★

Chapter 12

It was dark and cold and a hard wind was blasting off the Rockies when Jessie said the last words of a very brief eulogy. They all glanced at the young woman who stood as white and unmoving as a marble statue. Jessie wished the girl would cry or scream or do something. Anything rather than just stand there unmoving.

"She's blocked everything from her mind," Dr. Evans said, as they took the girl's arm and led her back to the coach. They helped the girl inside, and Ki insisted that he drive the team on down to Denver.

"It'll be better if you and the doctor stay inside with her," he said.

"Are you sure that you can handle the team?" Jessie asked.

Ki nodded. He had a thick leather coat and he would be fine. "It's time that I started doing something," he said. "My arm feels fine now. The cracked bones have mended and my head is clear. There is no numbness remaining."

"But you're still not well," Jessie fretted. "I've seen the way you sometimes lose your balance."

"Don't worry," Ki assured her. And then, to prove his point, the samurai climbed up on the driver's seat and took the lines. Looking back down at them, he said, "We'd better get moving. I've a feeling we are about to be hit by a rain squall."

Jessie and the doctor piled inside the coach, and Ki drove the team off. He felt much better up on the top and doing something useful. And while it was true that he was not back to normal, he could feel his well-conditioned body recovering. Ki was certainly not up to fighting men as big and as strong as the Hogan brothers, but in a few more days . . . well, perhaps he would be able to give a creditable account of himself.

It began to storm long before Ki saw the faint outline of Denver through the pelting rain. Because he and Jessie had visited this city many times and he was very familiar with its offerings, Ki drove straight to the Bedford Hotel.

Jessie and the doctor came tumbling out, slipping in the already muddy street. Overhead, thunder rumbled and crashed as shivering bolts of lightning struck the Rocky Mountain peaks just to the west.

"I'll get us rooms!" Jessie called, helping the young woman out and bustling her into the hotel.

Ki drove on through the hard rain. Steam lifted from the coats of the horses, and their hooves made loud, sucking sounds in the mud. He turned right on Larimer Street and drove straight through the massive open doors of the Denver Livery.

Moses Black was the longtime owner and proprietor. "Ki!" the old man shouted. He got up from a keg of horseshoes and grinned, showing that he had no teeth. "Damned if it ain't good to see you! Where's the most beautiful woman God ever put on this man's green earth?"

"Jessie is checking into the Bedford Hotel along with

some friends," Ki said, carefully climbing down from the carriage.

"Say, what's the matter with you?" Moses asked with a frown. "You break a leg or somethin'?"

"Or something," Ki said, not really in the mood to explain. He shook hands with Moses. "Where are your boys on a day like this?"

"At home in bed with their wimmen, I'd think," Moses said with a wink. "Leastways, if I wasn't so old and ugly, that's where I'd be."

"No woman would have an old mossy back like you," Ki said, recalling how much the man enjoyed a good teasing.

"Well, sir," Moses drawled, already starting to unhitch the carriage so that he could remove the harness from the steaming horses and rub them off with gunnysacks, "I guess that I am a little old and smelly. But I was smelling when I was your age and the wimmen didn't object so damn much."

Despite the fact that Ki was shaking with cold, he smiled. Moses Black was one of the real characters in this town and was as decent a human being as ever was to be found.

Ki helped the old man unharness the team and put them into the stalls. Once, Moses looked at him with concern and said, "You look plumb peaked, Ki. You sure you oughta be helpin' me instead of goin' to bed and restin'?"

"I'm sure," Ki said. "Have you seen a wagon come by driven by two huge men with black beards?"

"There's a lot of wagons go up and down Larimer Street driven by men with black beards."

"Well, these are really huge men. Giants."

"Naw, I ain't seen 'em. But hell, I don't stand out in front watchin' folks pass by. Maybe you ought to go try the other liveries."

"I will," Ki said. "I was just hoping since yours is the

biggest and best, that I'd get lucky."

Moses beamed. "How long are you and Jessie stayin' this time?"

"Depends on whether we find those men or not," Ki said. "If they didn't stop in Denver, then we'll be leaving for Santa Fe first thing in the morning."

Ki hurried off, and since Denver was not a huge town, he was able to visit every livery within the next hour. He returned to the Bedford Hotel wet and discouraged.

"No news?" Jessie asked.

"Uh-uh," Ki said. "Either they rolled right on through town, or they stopped and didn't bother to feed their team."

"They might have bought grain and a few supplies and then kept going," Jessie said, glancing at Dr. Evans and then the young woman. "We have to find her a place to stay before we leave tomorrow."

"I know," Evans said. "She is in no condition to travel with us. Especially since the weather has taken a turn for the worse."

But the young woman surprised them all by speaking for the first time. "They killed my family. I want to see them hang!"

Jessie, Ki and Dr. Evans were so astonished that their mouths dropped open. Evans was the first to react. "You remember?"

She stared at the doctor for so long that Jessie thought the girl's mind must have slipped away again. "I remember . . . graves." She turned to Jessie. "I remember you sayin' the Lord's Prayer and the wind was blowin' hard in my face. I remember a fire."

"Do you remember," the doctor said gently, "everything that happened?"

She looked at him with a blank expression. "I don't believe I know what you mean, sir."

"I'm asking if you remember who killed your family."

Her eyes filled with tears, and they began to slide down her cheeks. "No, sir, I do not," she said, swallowing hard. "I just remember the graves and the prayerful words."

Jessie glanced at the doctor. Evans cleared his own throat and said, "Miss . . . what is your name?"

"Nancy. Mrs. Nancy Spicer. I miss my husband somethin' awful."

Jessie went and enfolded the poor woman in her arms. "I'm sorry about your husband."

"He was a good man," she whispered. "We was on our way to a house we'd bought in Denver."

"We're in Denver now," Jessie said. "Do you remember where this place is?"

She nodded her head. "It's a pretty house with a picket fence and roses hangin' on the front porch. We was movin' down from the Dakotas. Had a dry-land farm but the winters were too hard."

Jessie looked to Ki and the doctor. "In the morning we'll settle her affairs. Find the house and an attorney who can make sure that she is taken care of."

"But she doesn't have anything," Evans protested. "And she's in no condition to be left to her own devices."

"You're right," Jessie admitted. "But we can't abandon the Lane brothers to their awful fates."

The girl looked up at Jessie. "I liked what you said about my family. I wanted to say something nice too, but I couldn't. I tried, but the words stuck in my throat and it hurt so bad that I couldn't say anything."

"I'm sure that they understood'," Jessie said.

A few minutes later, Jessie escorted the doctor and the samurai to her door and whispered, "I'll get Nancy settled into bed. If you're up to it, perhaps you could visit a few of the saloons and try to find out if the Hogan brothers were in town and where they might be now."

"Sure," Ki said.

Dr. Evans nodded. "It shouldn't take more than an hour or two."

"They might still be here," Jessie said. "We can't just assume that they've passed through. We've got to be certain that they are on the road to Santa Fe before we leave."

"What about her?" Evans asked.

"We'll make a decision tomorrow morning. By then, maybe she'll even remember."

Dr. Evans frowned. "Perhaps that wouldn't be such a good idea for a while, Jessie. What she went through is enough to cause her mind to slip permanently. She needs a little time."

"Time," Jessie said, "is one thing that we do not have. The Lane brothers are running out of it."

"I know."

Ki and the doctor hurried away then, and for the next hour they found no one that recalled seeing a pair of bearded giants fitting the description of Abe and Eli Hogan. But at the Blue Dog Saloon, their luck finally changed.

"I remember those gorillas," the bartender said. "We had to call the sheriff and it took him and three deputies to make them leave. Why, them boys are as mean as teased snakes! I told 'em never to come back."

"What did they do?"

"Got drunk . . . which is just fine. But then they got real nasty and started shootin' this place up."

The bartender pointed to the ceiling. "See all them bullet holes?"

Ki nodded.

"Well, all but a couple are on account of them two big bastards you're lookin' for. They broke Joe Fiddler's arms—both of 'em! And all poor Joe did was suggest

90

that they might be better off to find a different saloon to shoot up."

"They're a bad lot," Dr. Evans said. "Did you see or hear them say anything about their prisoners?"

"Prisoners?"

"According to them, they've been deputized and are authorized to return several men to Santa Fe."

The bartender shook his head. "I can't believe that any judge in his right mind would deputize a couple of sonsabitches like that! Why, they should have been hanged years ago!"

Ki nooded in agreement. "We're trying to figure out if they're still in Denver or if they've pulled their freight and continued on down to Santa Fe."

"My guess is that they've up and left," the bartender said. "Of course, you might want to ask Sheriff Turner. I reckon, after all the ruckus they caused, that the sheriff will have kept tabs on them. I heard him tell them straight out that they weren't welcome in this town and he wanted them out of here. But they were the kind that might just have stayed on account of they wouldn't back down from a pair of grizzly bears."

"I know what you mean," Evans said. "They are the kind that would just naturally do the opposite of what you told them."

"I hope I never see 'em again," the bartender declared, dragging a sawed-off shotgun out from under his bar. "If I do, I'll use this on 'em. I talked myself blue in the face the last time and it didn't amount to squat. They ain't the kind to listen to nothin' but the sight of the barrel of a gun pointed at their thick damn heads."

Ki and the doctor agreed. After they left the Blue Dog, they visited several other saloons, but no one else had seen or heard of the Hogan brothers.

91

Evans pulled out his pocket watch. "It's damn near eleven o'clock and I'm done in," he said. "Given your health, Ki, you shouldn't be doing all the things you've been asked today."

"I could use some sleep myself," the samurai conceded. "In the morning we can see Sheriff Turner and then we ought to know for sure if the Hogans are still in Denver."

As they walked slowly back toward the Bedford Hotel, the doctor said, "What do you think?"

"About what?"

"Are they still here?"

The samurai shrugged. "Do you think that Nancy will ever remember and be able to identify the men who killed her husband and parents?"

The doctor smiled sadly. "I can't answer that. My guess is that she will if she ever wants to regain peace of mind."

The next morning they were waiting at the sheriff's office when the man arrived with his deputy. "Can I help you folks?"

Jessie came right to the point. "We understand you had quite a bit of trouble with a pair of huge men in the Blue Dog Saloon the other night. The Hogan brothers?"

The sheriff nodded. "I told them to get out of town and stay out."

"Did they?"

"Yep."

Jessie pressed the question. "Are you absolutely sure?"

"Of course! One of my deputies saw them roll through town later that night. They were driving a high-sided wagon. Isn't that right, Wes?"

The deputy nodded.

"Thank you," Jessie said.

"What's this all about?"

92

In a few words, Jessie explained to the sheriff about the Hogan brothers and how they had taken the Lane brothers hostage. "We think it has something to do with a family feud down in New Mexico and property rights."

"Sounds like bad news for the Lanes," the sheriff replied. "Them big boys play real rough. I had to bring in every deputy I had on my payroll and even then—outnumbered three-to-one—they still were half-ready to let bullets fly."

"They're killers," Jessie said. "And by the way, we have a girl whose husband and family were murdered about twenty or thirty miles north of Denver."

"Murdered?"

"Yes. We buried the victims."

"You should have brought them in for identification," the sheriff said.

"There was a survivor. A young woman. She's staying at the Bedford and claims that her family had just bought a house in town."

"Did she say where?"

"No," Jessie answered, "but she thinks she can find it. My question is, do you know of someone who can help her? She's destitute and suffering from partial amnesia."

"Hmmm. Well," Turner said, "I could talk to some of the churchgoers. I'm sure that they would take up a collection or something."

"Nancy is going to need some kind of guardian. Someone who can take care of her legal and financial matters."

"I can give you some names," the sheriff said. "That's about all I can do, though. Sounds to me like she needs a lot of help."

"She does," Jessie said, "and I'd stay to see that Nancy had it only we have to rush on to Santa Fe."

"Of course."

"Thanks, Sheriff," Jessie said, sensing that the lawman

was going to be long on sympathy but short on actual help.

An hour later found them standing before a rather large and prominent house with a picket fence, roses and a wide veranda.

"This is it?" Jessie asked again.

"Yes, it is," Nancy said, smiling sadly to herself. "We were all going to share this home. It's pretty, isn't it?"

"Very," Jessie said as Nancy led them in through the front gate. All of Jessie's doubts disappeared when Nancy reached behind a loose board on the veranda and retrieved a key, which she used to open the door.

It was empty inside, but very well maintained, with high ceilings, lots of ornate woodwork and a winding staircase up to what Jessie supposed were bedrooms.

"It's a beautiful house," Dr. Evans said. "It kind of reminds me of the one I grew up in back east."

"It is nice," Nancy said, pirouetting around in a full circle. "I hope I can come back soon."

Jessie blinked. "What do you mean?"

"I've decided to go with you to Santa Fe," she said quietly.

"But . . . but you can't!"

"Maybe the men that you want are the same ones that killed my husband and parents," she explained. "I *must* come."

"It would be too much for you," Jessie argued.

"I'm coming," Nancy told them. "You can leave me behind if you want, but I'll get there even if I have to walk."

"Nancy, you just don't . . ."

But the young woman had turned away and was starting up the stairs. "I'll show you the bedrooms," she said. "They are very pretty."

Ki and Jessie exchanged worried glances. Ki said, "What will we do about her?"

"She means it," Jessie said. "I can't tell you how I know, but she does."

"Of course she does," Evans said. "Perhaps deep in her mind, she understands that she *has* to face those who killed her family and help bring them to justice in order to have any peace the remainder of her life."

"Then we should take her?" Jessie asked.

"I think we have to."

"Don't you want to see it?" Nancy called down from the upstairs landing. "The rooms are very pretty. My husband had our room painted rose pink, just because I so love that color."

Jessie started up the stairs, her mind churning. She did not want to take this poor young widow along. There might be hardships and trials that she could not even imagine in wait for them down in the New Mexico Territory. Also, they'd be in the Hogan's stomping grounds, where those awful men might well have the benefit of a corrupt judge and the wealth and power of their entire ranching family.

"What are we going to do now!" Evans whispered.

"We admire her bedroom," Jessie said. "And then we all head south for Santa Fe."

★

Chapter 13

As they neared the old Southern Colorado ranching and logging town of Three Rivers, Nate Lane knew that he was going to die if he did not get some help.

"You gotta stop and find me a doctor!" he shouted. "I'm on fire!"

Abe looked over his shoulder. "Then burn in hell!"

Nate looked to his brothers. "Either I get help, or I'll be dead by tonight. If I die, you gotta swear you won't help 'em to get our lands. You both gotta swear it!"

"Shut up!" Eli hissed.

Nate was wild with desperation. "I ain't going to shut up no more! Either you get me a doctor, or none of us will ever sign over our family property."

"Eli, did you just hear that?" Abe asked, pulling the team to a halt. He tied the lines and pivoted around on the seat to look back down into the bed of the wagon.

"I heard it," Eli said, drawing his pistol. He looked around at the tall trees. "I think I'll just put him out of his misery right now and we'll be done with this catawaulin'."

Eli cocked back the hammer of his six-gun and pointed it at a place between Nate's feverish eyes.

Orin cried, "You shoot him, you might as well shoot us too! We'll *never* sign over nothing! We'll scream and raise so much hell that you'll wish you never seen either of us again!"

"Hold it," Abe said to his brother. "Don't shoot. Not yet."

"Why the hell not!" Eli snapped. "I say we just shoot all three of 'em."

"Stop talking like a damned fool! We swore to Pa we'd bring them back alive."

"But we already kilt one."

"And that's enough," Abe said. "We promised to bring them back and we've almost done it. A couple more days and we'll be home."

Eli eased the hammer on his six-gun down and scowled. He was not pleased, but he dipped his chin in acknowledgment. "Nate is going to die anyway," he said. "Might as well shoot him and be done with it."

But Abe disagreed. "I say we find a doctor and let him have a look at that shoulder. If he can be saved, we ought to do that so we can tell Pa that we did the best we could to bring 'em in."

"Well, I ain't payin' for no doctorin' for Nate!"

"I will, then," Abe said, making his decision and turning back around to take up the lines. "I'll find him a doctor. If he's so far gone that he dies anyway, at least we can claim we tried to save him like we promised. A man can't do much more than that."

Eli angrily jammed his gun into his holster. "I don't know what in the hell is gettin' to be the matter with you," he swore. "Used to be if you needed to kill a man, you just up and killed him and didn't give it a second thought. Now,

97

it's all different. I'm beginnin' to think maybe you've lost your gumption."

Abe spat a stream of tobacco at the ground. "Brother," he rumbled, "don't you ever make the mistake of thinkin' that I'm gonna one day be your second fiddle. I have always been able to whip your ass and I always will."

Eli's lips curled like those of a dog fixin' to growl. But he didn't say a thing because, gumption or not, Abe was still his big brother. "I hope this damn town ain't even got a doctor," he hissed.

Hoot Anderson was the town dentist, doctor and mortician. He did none of those individual tasks particularly well, but he did them all just well enough to eke out a life of relative ease. Hoot's passion wasn't serving mankind. It was fishing, whiskey drinking and womanizing. Lately, however, the whiskey had been bothering his digestion and the fishing in the three little streams that gave the town its name had not been too damn good, either. That left only womanizing to enjoy, and Hoot was thankful because it was his favorite of the three.

When the two giants stepped into the shabby little room where he conducted his meager business, Hoot was playing solitaire and daydreaming about a dance hall girl who had recently moved to Three Rivers. Her name was Shirley, and she was a little chubby, but still handsome. Besides, a real looker would not have had any interest in a man who had little ambition, a receding hairline and a wallet thinner than a whisker.

"We hear that you're the only damn doctor in Three Rivers!" Abe growled.

"Not much of a doctor," Hoot replied, not liking the looks of these men and wondering which one was ailing.

"Well, we ain't got much of a patient, either," Eli said, cackling at his own joke. "Son of a bitch is about dead."

"Where is he?"

"Out in the wagon with the other prisoners we're delivering to Santa Fe. You wanna have a look-see at him?"

Hoot did not. He'd gotten stuck twice before after doctoring prisoners, and he wasn't about to have it happen to him a third time.

"I guess I don't."

"He's gonna die if you don't help him," Abe said. "What the hell kind of a doctor you supposed to be?"

"Like I said, not much."

Abe glared at Hoot, and Eli said, "I guess you'll doctor our prisoner anyway."

"Now wait just a damn. . ." Hoot's protest died on his lips as both giants pulled Bowie knives from behind their belts, and it was damned obvious that they weren't fixing to use them to pick their teeth. "Uh . . . fine. Bring him in."

"Be easier if you came out and doctored him in the wagon," Abe said, clearing a way to the door.

Hoot nodded and left his unfinished hand of solitaire on the table. He followed the men outside, and when they lowered the back of the wagon and he saw the wretched condition of the three Lane brothers, he was shocked.

"By God, they're in awful shape!" he exclaimed, staring into the pain-stricken eyes of Nate and his younger brothers, whose faces were still purplish and distorted.

"Two of 'em will live, it's that 'un with the bad shoulder that needs the doctorin'."

"I. . . I'm not qualified to take care of men in this condition."

"You're the only chance he's got. You wanna tell him that you're gonna turn your back on him, go right ahead," Abe said.

Hoot gulped. Sweat beaded on his forehead though the

day was cool and overcast. He thought he'd never seen three such miserable creatures in his life, be they man or beast.

"What's the matter with his shoulder?" he heard himself ask.

"Bullet. Was removed by a doc already but it didn't heal clean. Looks pretty bad and he's in awful pain."

"And what about these other two! Why, their faces have been battered almost beyond recognition!"

"They had to be taught lessons," Eli said. Then he added with a bark of laughter, "They ain't very quick learners."

Hoot felt a shiver of fear. "I can't do anything here in the wagon," he stammered. "I'll need to treat them in my office, not out in the cold."

Eli and Abe exchanged glances, and something must have passed between them because it was Abe who finally nodded. "All right. You got saloons close by?"

"Three or four just up the street."

"How long will you need?"

"I can't say yet," Hoot stammered. "Maybe two hours."

"Two hours?" Abe growled, his brow furrowing with disapproval.

"Maybe a little less," Hoot added quickly. "I . . . I can't rightly say. I haven't even seen the man's shoulder yet."

"I'll fix that," Eli said, hopping into the wagon, stepping over Orin and Jeb to grab Nate by the shirtfront and haul him to his feet.

"Ahhh!" Nate cried out with pain.

"Easy on that man!" Hoot ordered, outraged at such insensitivity. "Bring him inside."

"Well," Abe said, "as you can plainly see, if one comes, they all come since they're chained and shackled together."

"How long have they been forced to live like this!"

100

"Since we caught 'em pannin' gold in the Feather River."

Hoot shook his head and turned away. He did not trust himself to speak, for fear he'd anger the giants, who might then kill them all.

"Bring them along," Hoot said. "They all need attention."

When the three brothers were brought inside, they were so weak and emaciated that they could barely stand.

"Sit them down there on that bench," Hoot ordered, shaking his head and trying to ignore the stench of unwashed bodies and rotting flesh.

He moved over to Nate. The man could barely hold his head up. Hoot unbuttoned Nate's shirt, and when he saw the infected shoulder, he recoiled. "My God," he whispered.

"Can you do anything for him?"

"I doubt God Hisself could at this point."

"Then we'll just put 'em back in the wagon and soon be on our way," Eli said.

"No!" Hoot lowered his voice. "I mean, I might be able to do something for the shoulder. But now that I've seen it, I think it'll take longer than I originally thought. This man ought to be hospitalized."

"Maybe we could give you overnight," Abe said. "I could do with a bath and a woman! You got whores in this town, ain't ya?"

Hoot thought of Shirley. "There are a few girls working the saloons," he snapped.

"How much they ask fer it?" Eli demanded.

"I don't know."

"Hell yes, you do! How much?"

"Couple of dollars," Hoot said, not meeting their eyes.

"Fer that kind of money, they'll have to work hard," Abe rumbled. "Let's go."

101

"Wait!" The giants turned at the door. "I can't doctor this man's shoulder if his wrists are handcuffed behind his back!"

"Why the hell not?"

"Because I may have to do some cutting of flesh!"

The two brothers exchanged glances again. "All right," Abe said, "but we leave the ankle clamps on and they stay chained together. You take good care of 'em until we come back later. You do anything wrong, you're gonna hurt worse'n any of 'em. Understand me?"

Hoot nodded. "What . . . what did they do to deserve this kind of treatment?"

"They're murderers!" Eli cried. "They cut the hearts out of Santa Fe women and ate 'em!"

Hoots eyes widened. "No!"

"It's a fact," Abe said. "And if you ain't careful, they'll kill you, too."

Hoot stared at the Lane brothers. He didn't believe a word of it. And as for hurting him, he thought that ridiculous. These men could not hurt anyone. They were too weak and in too much pain.

Abe removed the handcuffs from Nate's wrists, and then he and his brother sauntered up the street to find whiskey and women. When Hoot was sure that they were gone, he grabbed Nate by the chin and shook his head.

"Who are they!"

Nate was almost delirious, but his brothers were able to answer Hoot's question. They told him about their family ranch lands and the feud that had gradually reduced the number of men in their family down to a few old ones and themselves; told how they'd fled for their lives in the hope that they might be able to find new land or even some placer gold in the California Gold Rush country along the western slopes of the Sierras.

102

"The only reason they're keeping us alive is so we can sign over our ranch lands. That's the only reason."

Hoot believed them. "It's probably too late, but I do have some medicine that might help save your life," he told Nate Logan.

"Much obliged," Nate whispered. "Much obliged."

"And I might have to cut some of the rotting flesh away. The surgery might kill you, but I don't know what else I can do."

"Go ahead," Nate breathed. "Do whatever you can. I ain't afraid of dyin'. I'd almost welcome it."

Hoot believed the man. He had never seen such suffering, and he'd seen a lot of men very near death. He went to a little cabinet and removed a quart jar of whiskey. "Here," he aid, putting the bottle to Nate's lips. "Drink all you want."

Nate's eyes fluttered open, and when he saw the whiskey bottle, he raised one hand and clutched it as a dying nun would her crucifix. He drank in big, shuddering gulps until he choked.

"Here," Hoot said, helping the other two brothers drink their fill.

It was amazing how whiskey could restore a man's color in just a few moments. Hoot took several long pulls of his own, and then he set to work paring away the rotting flesh. He packed the terrible wound with a dressing that he'd used successfully in the past.

He turned his attention to Orin and Jeb, examining their faces and applying a medicinal ointment. "You poor bastards look like you've been beaten with clubs."

"Fists," Jeb said. "You gonna help us get away from them, Doc?"

"Hell no! They'd catch and kill us all."

"They're gonna kill us anyway" Orin said. "We got nothin' to lose."

103

"Well, I got *plenty* to lose," Hoot snapped, "starting with my life."

"You let them take us on to Santa Fe, you're gonna sentence us to a hard death."

"It's none of my affair."

"It should be," Orin said. " 'Cause it's worse'n murder. That's what it is."

Hoot knew they were telling him the truth. "I don't even know where I could take you," he said. "Besides, your brother can't be moved."

"Yes, Nate can. And you can take us in that wagon outside."

"That's their wagon!"

"No it ain't. They stole it in Cheyenne. It's yours to take."

"I don't want to hear this. Any of it!" Hoot wanted to cover his ears like a child.

Orin sniffled. "Then you might just as well be savin' that medicine you're puttin' on our faces. Might just as well be trying to heal a couple of corpses."

Hoot turned away, wanting to run, just run away from these three poor bastards and stay away until they were gone. Then, he'd sit back down with his hand of solitaire and life would go back to normal, the way it had been just an hour ago, and maybe next year the fishing would improve.

"Mister?"

"What!"

"You *gotta* help us," Jeb whispered. "You're the last and only chance we got."

Hoot turned around to face the pair. "What do you think I could possibly do against two monsters like those that brought you to me?"

"Just turn us loose. Let us take the wagon and get up

into the mountains where they can't find us."

"What about me! I'm not any more ready to die than you are."

Jeb swallowed. "You could hide, too, I reckon. You must know some place hereabouts! Or . . . or maybe someone who'd help you."

For some crazy reason, Hoot thought of Shirley. She had a little shack behind the Golden Spike Saloon. He knew she would help, no matter what the risks to her own life.

"Mister, if you help us and somehow we get to keep our land, I swear we'll repay you," Orin said. "I'll swear it on any Bible you might want me to lay my hand on. I swear—"

"All right!"

Hoot blinked. He hadn't meant to agree to this. He hadn't meant to at all. The words had just jumped out of his mouth.

Dammit! He should have locked his door today and just gone fishing, even if they weren't biting anymore.

★

Chapter 14

"The very first thing we have to do is get the hell out of here fast!" Hoot said. "If Three Rivers had a sheriff, that's where we'd run. But since it don't, we'll just run."

"But where!"

"I know someone that might help." Hoot was not a big man or a particularly strong one, but his adrenaline was flowing, so he picked Nate up and said, "It's finally getting dark outside. We can leave the back way."

Hoot knew he was insane to be doing this; he had everything to lose and nothin to gain. Three Rivers was damn small, and if the Hogan brothers really wanted to recapture these poor shackled sonsabitches, they could search every building in the whole town.

As they hurried along the alley, Hoot knew that they could never escape as long as these three were chained and shackled, wrist and ankle. "The blacksmith will help us," he said. "We've *got* to get those off or we're finished."

Jeb was struggling hard and barely able to move along because he was in such bad shape.

"Help your brother!" Hoot told Orin. "I've already got my hands full with Nate."

It seemed to Hoot that it took at least an hour to reach the blacksmith's shop. By that time, they were bathed in sweat despite the cold night air. Hoot's heart was pounding so hard he thought it might explode. "Sam, you got to get these shackles off of 'em!"

Sam Garrett was not pleased. "Hellfire! If they're prisoners, I could get in big trouble."

"They're innocent," Hoot argued. "If I didn't believe that, I wouldn't be risking my own life. Please, Sam, just cut them loose and we won't say a word about you."

"But I'm the only damn blacksmith in Three Rivers! They're gonna know who did it."

"Listen," Hoot said, aware that he was pleading. "Why don't you just ride off for a day or two until this all blows over?"

"I don't know," Sam hedged. "I can't see that there's a damn thing in it for me."

"Yes, there is," Orin said in a pleading voice. "We got a ranch. Maybe . . . maybe you could have a stake in it! I can't speak for my whole family, but—"

"Aw, hell!" Sam groused. "I don't want to take land clear down in the New Mexico Territory. Besides, I'm just a blacksmith. I don't know nothin' about ranchin'."

"We're innocent," Orin said. "I swear to God that we're innocent."

They could see Sam's resolve wavering.

"Help us," Hoot begged. "Please. All you got to do is free them up and then leave town for a day or two until this passes."

"All right, dammit," Sam growled. "Come on in and let's get this over with so all of us can get out of here before them deputies come searchin'."

107

When the blacksmith had them lined up beside his anvil, he took less than a minute to inspect the handcuffs and then he picked up his hammer and a tempered steel chisel. "Boys, just close your eyes and don't move!"

Orin's handcuffs were the first to feel the blacksmith's chisel. Hoot saw the chisel's hard steel bite deep into the softer metal of the cuffs. A second blow drove the chisel through cleanly.

Orin sagged with relief, but the blacksmith said, "That's just half of it. Let's get rid of those leg shackles."

The leg shackles proved no more of an obstacle than the handcuffs. Jeb was next and then Nate, who was still unconscious.

"Is he dyin'?" Sam asked.

"I don't know," Hoot replied. "I think he's still got a chance. They already removed his handcuffs. All you need to do is break the leg iron."

Sam positioned Nate's leg on his anvil and said, "If I was to miss just a quarter inch on either side, I'd sever his artery. He'd die easy instead of sufferin'."

Hoot's voice hardened. "I'm no real doctor, but I say he's got a chance, so don't play God and miss!"

Sam nodded. "I was just supposin'," he said, raising his hammer and slamming it down on the chisel. The leg iron broke as easy as an eggshell.

Sam was pleased. "I figured that it would go through in one whack if I really put the arm to 'er."

Hoot threw Nate across his shoulder and said, "Thanks, Sam! I owe you a tooth extraction or whatever. Now hide those shackles and get out of here before them big deputies come asking questions!"

"I'll do it," Sam promised. "Where you goin' to hide?"

"Better you don't know," Hoot said, turning and disappearing into the night.

• • •

At first, Hoot had intended simply to take the Hogan brothers wagon to make their escape. But then he realized that the deputies would easily be able to follow the tracks. Now, he was thinking that he would ask Shirley to hide them until all this trouble blew over. Shirley was a good woman with a kind heart despite what she had to do to earn a living.

"Are you sure she'll help us?" Orin asked as they stood outside her back door.

"I'm sure," Hoot said, praying that Shirley wasn't still singing and dancing at the Golden Spike.

"Who is it!" a groggy voice called from inside.

Hoot's spirits soared. "Shirley, it's me, Hoot!"

"Hoot?"

"Hoot Anderson. You know, the doc!"

There was a long silence, and then Shirley said, "Go away, Hoot! I got company."

Hoot took a half step backward. "Company?"

"Please! Can't you just come back later?"

Hoot swallowed his disappointment. He'd been a damn fool to think that Shirley was spending her nights alone. And now, he was in a real fix.

"Sure," he mumbled.

"What are we gonna do now?" Orin asked nervously. "Every minute we lose is killin' off our chances."

"I know that, dammit!" Hoot swore, wishing he had some whiskey to drink.

For a wild moment, he even considered returning to his office and digging his old cap-and-ball revolver out of his drawer and holding these three wretches under guard until the Hogan brothers returned. He could claim that . . . that what? The moment those giants saw that the handcuffs and shackles had been removed, they'd know the truth and kill him.

"Well, we can't just stay here!" Jeb cried. "I say we steal some horses and—"

"No!" Hoot lowered his voice. "If we did that, we could all be hanged for thievin'. That's not the way."

"Well then, what the hell is!"

Hoot did not know. His mind seemed paralyzed with fear and indecision. Inwardly he cursed himself for being so stupid as to get mixed up in this affair. By God, this could be the death of him if he didn't start thinking and thinking fast.

"Let's go to my house," he heard himself say. "I've got a couple of pistols there and two rifles. Maybe we'll just have to ambush them big bastards when they come looking for us."

"Okay," Orin said, glancing at Jeb, who barely had the strength to walk. "If that's what we have to do, then let's do it!"

They began hurrying back up the alley. They were just fifty or sixty feet behind Hoot's office when the heard the crack of furniture and breaking glass. Hoot jumped into the deepest shadows with Nate still draped over his shoulder.

"I'll skin that miserable sonofabitchin' doctor alive!" came the shout, punctuated by more breaking furniture and glass.

"Let's torch this son of a bitch!"

Hoot's eyes widened a few minutes later as he saw flames through his windows. "They're burning me out," he whispered.

"I'm sorry, Doc," Orin said. "But if you get us through this, we'll make it up to you. I swear we will."

"Sure," he said, not believing a word of it.

"We still goin' to your house?"

"I don't think so," he heard himself say. "That's about the first place they'll go looking now that we're gone."

110

"Then what. . . ."

Hoot rubbed his face. "I keep a horse in a little pasture just a few blocks north at the end of town. There's a few others with him and they're all dog gentle. I got the key to the lock of a tack room some of us share. We'll saddle those gentle horses and head for the high country."

"No," Orin argued, "let's head north! They'd never expect that."

But Hoot shook his head. "I know this old mountain man who has a cabin. It's hard to find and I'm sure he'll help us out."

"Like that whore just did?"

Hoot ignored the sarcastic remark and said, "We can wait this thing out. They won't keep hunting forever."

"I don't know," Orin said doubtfully. "They tracked us all the way to California. Took 'em better than a year. I'm thinkin' they won't stop no matter where we run."

"What have I got myself into?" Hoot said, watching as the flames leapt higher and higher from his office windows. They heard the ring of the town's fire alarm, signaling the arrival of the volunteer fire department, of which Hoot was a senior member.

"Don't you think we better be gettin' those horses?" Orin asked nervously.

Hoot shifted Nate on his shoulder, then reached down to check the man's pulse, half hoping that Nate was dead and could be left behind, so they could travel faster. But Nate clung stubbornly to life, and Hoot turned his back on his burning office and struck out for the north end of town. He and the brothers caught and saddled four horses, three of them belonging to friends who would not press charges against Hoot for borrowing their animals in an emergency. It was all Hoot could do to hoist Nate across the saddle and lash him down.

"If he survives this, he ought to be written up in the medical journals," Hoot muttered, mounting his horse and gazing up at the moon and stars.

"How far is that old mountain man's cabin?" Orin asked.

Hoot forgot to answer when he saw a figure emerge from the darkness. His blood froze until he realized that the silhouette was not nearly large enough to be one of the Hogan brothers.

"Hoot?"

"Shirley?"

She hurried forward. "I remembered you telling me about your horse. When I heard the fire bell ring I went out and saw it was your office. I heard those awful deputies were looking to arrest you."

"Arrest me?" Hoot chuckled but there was no mirth in it. "Shirley, they'd be more likely to skin me alive. If they catch us, we're goners."

"Where are you going?"

"I . . . I'm not sure," he lied, not willing to trust her again.

She touched his leg. "Hoot, I'm sorry. You came to me for help and I failed you."

"Forget it," he said roughly. "Now you better—"

"I can still help."

"It's too late."

"No! I can sneak you food and anything else you need."

"Why?"

She cleared her throat. "Because I was the one that you came to when you needed help."

"So?"

"So that means you trusted me with your life."

"We don't need her!" Orin said, his voice panicky. "Let's ride."

But Shirley's hand tightened on Hoot's leg. "I want to

112

help! That man I was with when you came tonight, he doesn't mean anything. It was just money."

Pride made Hoot want to tell Shirley to go to hell, tell her that he'd been a damn fool to put her on a pedestal, to think that she was any better than any other girl he'd ever known who danced in a saloon. But when Hoot looked down at her face, a little too plump, a little too hard but still pretty, all he could do was to nod his head.

"You see that saddle in the ridge up yonder?" he said, pointing toward the mountains. "That one with a little patch of snow?"

"Yes."

"If you can get there without anyone knowing, bring whatever goods you can."

She stared at the ridge. "How long a ride will it be?"

"Four, maybe five hours. There's a good trail leading off from it just a half mile south. I'll meet you there this time tomorrow night."

"Do you promise?"

"If I'm still alive, I do," he said, reining his horse away and forcing himself not to look back.

"I'll be there! I'll be there, Hoot!" she called through the darkness.

Hoot didn't say anything and he didn't look back. He'd believe her if she showed but not a minute sooner.

Chapter 15

"Burn the doc's house down too!" Abe roared. "And then we'll scout every inch of this two-bit town until we find them!"

Eli batted a kerosene lamp off a table. It spilled on the hardwood floor, then seeped into the clutter of old magazines and papers. "This place will go up like a torch," he said, striking a match and tossing it on the floor.

The fire made a whooshing sound and its flames spread quietly. "There's another lamp over there!" Abe shouted, pointing toward the bedroom window.

Eli lit a second fire. The flames raced up the window curtains and curled along the ceiling. Paint bubbled and burst.

"Let's get out of here!" Abe shouted.

"Grab those rifles!" Eli called, searching frantically through Hoot's drawers in the hope of discovering valuables. When he didn't find anything except a few old Mexican coins, one silver dollar and a nearly worthless black powder pistol, he cussed and left on his brother's heels.

"Where do we start?" Eli asked.

"My guess is that they can't get very far in shackles and chains. If I was them, my first stop would be the blacksmith's shop."

Eli nodded in agreement. They hurried up the street, watching as the volunteer fire department attempted to get the office fire under control before the flames jumped to the next building and threatened the entire business section of Three Rivers.

Then, someone shouted that Hoot Anderson's house was afire. Abe and his brother passed right on through the confusion until they reached the blacksmith shop, where a boy of about fifteen was standing by himself, staring at the conflagration. He was thin, barefooted and wearing a pair of patched bib overalls.

"Hey, boy!"

At the sound of Abe's voice, the kid whirled around, and his eyes widened with fear when he saw the size of the men who were confronting him.

"Yes, sir?"

"Is your pa the smithy in this town?"

"No, sir."

"Where can we find the man that owns this blacksmith shop?"

"He's fighting the fire."

"Which one is he?"

The boy pointed Sam out. "Old fella with the floppy hat."

Abe's eyes narrowed. "Did you see the doc and three other man come here tonight?"

"No, sir! I jest came to watch the fire."

Abe sensed that the boy wasn't clever enough to lie. "Run along!"

The boy ran. When he had gone, Abe spied a lantern. Lighting it before he stepped into the shop, he said, "Let's take a look inside and see if they've been here already."

Holding the lantern aloft, Abe surveyed the shop's interior. He walked past the huge bellows and kegs of various sizes of iron bars used to make horseshoes, branding irons and tools, and then he paused and knelt beside the anvil to run his fingers through the loose dirt.

"What are you doin' that for?"

"Thought I might find one of the links off our chain," Abe said, eyes settling on a big iron tub of water. It was just such a tub that the blacksmith used to douse and cool his red-hot horseshoes after they had been worked into the desired shape.

"You know what a blacksmith always does with pieces of iron he throws away?"

"No."

"He throws 'em into that tub of water," Abe said, plunging his right arm right up to the armpit in the deep tub, while still holding aloft the lantern.

"Ah-ha!" he cried, pulling up a fistful of handcuffs, leg irons and chain. "Guess where these came from?"

Eli swore with great passion. "So, they're loose now."

"Yep."

"Let's go get that blacksmith!"

"No," Abe said, "let's let him come to us."

"But—"

Abe's lips pulled down at the corners, and he hurled the lantern at the wall. It exploded in flames, and the Hogan brothers watched it for a moment before they stepped outside and walked a few yards up the street to stand in the shadows of another building.

It took almost five minutes for the flames to come licking out of the front door and the heat to shatter the windows. It was about another three minutes before someone up the street turned to see the new fire and shout an alarm to the already overtaxed fire fighters.

116

Men came racing across the street, many with buckets in their hands, sloshing over with water. One of the men was the blacksmith. Abe nodded to his brother, and Eli moved through the crowd as if he were coming to help form a new bucket brigade. Only instead, he slipped his Bowie knife from his belt and jammed it into the blacksmith's side.

Abe smiled to see the blacksmith stiffen, then quickly leave the other fire fighters, walking like a man being pulled on a set of puppet strings.

They dragged Sam into the darkest shadows. The black-smith was shaking with terror.

"Where did they go after you freed 'em of their shackles and chains?" Abe asked very quietly.

The man's head began to wag back and forth. "I don't know what you're talking about! I swear I don't."

"Jar his memory," Abe said, easy as could be.

Eli jammed the point of his knife a quarter inch deeper into the blacksmith's side. When a scream formed in Sam's throat, Abe stopped it with the knuckles of his fist. Sam collapsed on the ground, and Eli knelt at the blacksmith's side.

"One last time. Where did they go after you removed them chains and shackles?"

"I . . . I don't know! Please! You're killin' me!"

"You got that right," Eli said, drawing his blade hard against the blacksmith's throat, so the poor man began to strangle and drown in his own blood.

"Let's start turnin' this town upside down now that we got everyone's attention on the fire," Abe said.

They hurried away, leaving the blacksmith to die.

By dawn the fires were extinguished and fear had been replaced by outrage among the people of Three Rivers. Until then no one had had time to waste asking how or why the fires had been started. All that had mattered was that they had finally been halted, but not before they had claimed nearly a third of the downtown office buildings, including two popular saloons.

With dawn and the end of the threat, questions were on everyone's lips, and when they learned that the Hogan brothers had not only set the fires but then systematically searched every house, every business and every building in Three Rivers—while helping themselves to whatever valuables were in plain sight — the townspeople were incensed.

"Sam is murdered!" came the awful cry just after first light. "His throat has been cut!"

Men who had been grumbling and threatening action suddenly raced over to stare at the dead blacksmith.

"He musta died real hard from the looks of his face," Bert Wheeler, the honorary mayor said, gulping noisily.

Winfred Evans, the town's part-time gunsmith, pulled a Colt revolver from his holster and shouted, "I say we hunt them big boys down and string 'em up! I say this calls for rope justice!"

Men, sweaty from the fire's heat and with faces scorched and blackened, took up the call to arms. Those that had guns yanked them out and brandished them with threats of retribution, while those that had left their guns at home ran to get them, begging that the hunt for the giants be postponed for just a few minutes, please!

The crowd, leaderless and unfocused, swirled about aimlessly. It fed upon its own fury, seething and frothing. Then it began to surge up and down the smokey main street, searching for the Hogan brothers. Back and forth it went, opening the very same doors that Abe and Eli had already opened, peering in every crook and cranny, no matter how small.

"They're gone!" a man cried. "They musta left town!"

118

The people were outraged. They fired their weapons into the air. At least six had hangman's nooses, and these were waved overhead in anger.

"Let's form a posse!" a man shouted. "Let's saddle up and go hunt them down!"

"But where! We don't have any damned idea which way they went!"

"Where the hell did Doc go!"

"Were they really after him?"

The crowd became embroiled in a heated debate that went on and on. The sun rose higher and the day grew warm. By mid-morning the heat had all been talked and walked out of the men of Three Rivers. They surveyed the remains of their town, some thankful that they had been spared, others openly weeping over their losses.

And then they drifted off to be alone or with their families, and instead of revenge, they were thinking good luck to poor Doc, and good riddance to them goddamn murdering giants.

★

Chapter 16

Hoot Anderson had taken the Lane brothers up the South Fork of Willow Creek. They had ridden in the creek wherever possible, in the hope of washing out any sign of their escape. Orin felt it had been a waste of time and effort.

"Them Hogan brothers will find our tracks," he glumly predicted. "It might take 'em a week or even a month, but as long as it don't rain or snow, they'll pick up our tracks."

Hoot remembered that prediction as he moved higher and higher into the Rocky Mountains. All morning they kept crossing and recrossing the creek, and then, just after high noon, they struck out across a patch of loose gravel rock and took a steep game trail over a ridge into a high forest meadow.

"There's where we'll be staying for the next day or two," Hoot said, reining his horse to a standstill and pointing down to the mountain man's log cabin.

"Anybody living there right now?" Orin asked.

"I can't say for sure, but I hope he's still here. These old fellas are pretty restless. We'll just have to ride down and see."

"Looks deserted to me," Jeb said. "I don't see no horses or nothin'."

Hoot clucked his tongue and sent his own horse forward. He'd been to this place about six months before, and there had been an old recluse named Crazy Luke living here, panning Willow Creek near where it fed into the small alpine lake. He and Crazy Luke had taken an immediate liking to each other, and the old prospector had invited him back anytime he had a hankering.

"Stay lined out behind me," Hoot ordered, guiding his horse down the ridge and into the meadow. "Crazy Luke might get a little trigger happy if he sees all of us coming at once. I got a feeling his eyesight is failing and he might not even recognize me."

Even as Hoot said this, they heard the crack of a rifle and Hoot's Stetson went spinning into the sky.

"Hold it right there, boys!" a raspy voice called. "Jest turn them horses around and hightail it on out of here!"

"Hey, Luke! It's me, Hoot Anderson! Remember?"

There was a moment of silence, then a tall, buckskin-clad man, with a long mane of silver hair and a beard to match, stepped out from behind a tree. Crazy Luke's face was tobacco-juice brown, so dark and wrinkled that he looked like some old Indian chief. Besides the rifle, he was packing a pair of dueling pistols, stuffed behind a beaded Indian belt, and a Bowie knife fitted nicely into a sheath strapped to his lean but muscular thigh.

"Well, I'll be damned," Luke said, lowering his rifle. "Is that you, Hoot?" Luke grinned, and you could see why people mistook the old man for being crazy. A knife fight had once severed the muscles on the left side of his face, so that his grin was all cockeyed. One corner of his mouth lifted normally, but the other twisted downward. The result was that Luke grinned like a complete lunatic.

Hoot relaxed. "Yes, it's me all right. How are the fish bitin' these days, old-timer?"

"They's bitin' about like usual. But you know I ain't no damn fish lover. I got bear meat and venison. I eats rabbit and squirrel, too! Are your friends fish eaters, Hoot?"

Hoot's eyes followed those of the old man to the three brothers. "No, Luke, these men are being hunted by two giants that mean to kill us."

Luke studied on that for a minute. He walked over to Nate, who was unconscious. "It appears that this one is about kilt already, Hoot. Bad-lookin' shoulder."

"I know." Hoot dismounted and signaled for Orin and Jeb to do the same. "Luke, I was hoping you might help us out for a couple of days. Maybe you could even use some of your Indian medicines on Nate's shoulder. As you can see, that bullet poisoned his blood."

"Let's get him inside," Luke said, turning away and starting off toward his cabin. "Let's make some Ute medicine for him and see what happens."

Hoot nodded. He'd used the white man's medicine and while it had helped, he also set a big store by the Indian herbal medicines and potions. "Give me a hand, boys."

"Stretch him out on the table," Luke ordered when they were inside.

When they had managed that, the old man moved over beside Nate and studied his pale face. He placed his hand on Nate's throat and then his other hand on Nate's heart. Luke closed his eyes as if listening, and he was silent for so long that Orin blurted, "What are you doin'?"

Luke opened his eyes. "I'm feelin' for his life force. Seein' if this man has the will to live or if he just wants to die. If a man is hurt bad enough to want to die, I wouldn't try to call him back."

"Nobody *wants* to die," Orin said.

Luke studied Orin's battered face. "Some do. Some pray for death—some just kill themselves to be done with sufferin'. You boys have suffered aplenty. The men tryin' to kill you must be hard men."

"As hard as they come," Hoot said.

"Will they follow your tracks?"

Hoot wanted to lie but heard himself say, "I believe they will. It's just a matter of time."

Luke studied the three of them for several seconds; then he said, "Maybe we will kill them when they come to shed our blood, if they don't kill us first."

"I'd like that fine," Orin said. "Jeb, wouldn't you like that?"

"Well, sure, but—"

Luke said, "Your brother's spirit is very weak."

"Not his spirit, old man," Orin said defensively. "Nate is a fighter if ever there was one—it's his body that's about to give out because of all the hurtin' he's suffered. Mister Luke, he *wants* to live."

Luke passed a hand over Nate's face and felt the unconscious man's breath on it. "I will do what I can to save him."

"Much obliged," Orin said.

"But you will all have to leave. Go outside and wait, for now I have to make Indian medicine."

Orin objected. "But can't we stay and watch? He's our brother."

"Go," the old mountain man said, his voice rising with anger.

A second protest formed in Orin, but Hoot grabbed his arm and that of his younger brother and dragged them both outside.

"I don't see what the hell is wrong with us stayin' in there with him!" Orin cried when they were outside. "Hell, I feel

123

like it's our right to watch and make sure he doesn't give Nate some kind of Injun poison."

"I feel the same," Jeb said. "You're a doctor. How come you're not stickin' with our brother?"

"I've done what I can for Nate," Hoot explained. "I've cut out his rotting flesh and cleaned the wound. But Nate still has a fever and there's nothing more I can do. Poison has spread through his body. I don't have any medicines for that kind of thing, but Luke does."

"Injun medicines?" Orin scoffed. "What kind of doctor are you to allow Injun medicines?"

"I'm not a real doctor," Hoot confessed. "But I do have a knack for treating others and I've read some. Anybody out west knows that Indian medicines can sometimes work miracles when everything else fails."

Orin and Jeb weren't convinced, but when Hoot went to hobble the horses and then unsaddle them so that they could graze in the meadow, they followed along.

Two hours before sundown, Hoot resaddled his weary horse and rode off to see if Shirley had actually come up from Three Rivers as promised to bring them food. Hoot wished that he had not asked the woman to risk her life, and he would not have if he'd been sure that Crazy Luke was still at this place. But he *had* asked and now he would be there as he promised, even if it did pose a serious risk.

At sundown, he dismounted and tied his horse to a tree, right beside the patch of snow he'd pointed out to the dance hall woman the night before.

"She ain't comin'," he grumbled. "She's either dancin' or screwin' somebody for a couple of dollars."

But Shirley did come. She rode her pony out from behind a jumble of rocks and said, "You sure had me worried, Hoot Anderson. I figured that you might have changed your mind

124

and were already halfway to California."

Hoot grinned and helped the woman down from her horse. "If I had any sense, I would be long gone."

She clung to him. "And why am *I* here? That's the question I can't answer."

Hoot crushed the woman in his arms and kissed her. When she squirmed and kissed him even harder, he lowered her to the ground, and as he pushed her dress up around her hips and she fumbled to unloosen his belt, she whispered, "I thought you wanted food."

"I did," he said, finally getting her underclothes pulled down and his own pants dropped to his knees.

She squirmed under him, getting her dress up a little higher and opening her legs wide. As he rammed his stiff rod into her, she gasped and then pushed her tongue into his ear. It made Hoot go wild. This was the fastest, craziest thing he'd ever done in his life, screwing this woman right here on an open, wet hillside next to a patch of snow.

But screw her he did and with more energy than he'd believed he still possessed. Their lovemaking was frantic until they both shouted with pleasure and their bodies stiffened with release. It was the most satisfying union Hoot had ever known.

For long minutes, as the sun died on the peaks just a few hundred feet above them, their bodies remained locked together. Finally, Hoot rolled off the woman. He stood and pulled up his pants, unsure of what he wanted to say, or do.

"Hoot?"

He looked down at her. "Yeah?"

"It was different . . . wasn't it?"

"Yeah. A whole lot different."

"How come?"

"I don't know. Maybe being half scared out of my mind this last day or so . . . well, maybe I had to empty all the fear out of me."

"Into me?" she asked. "I don't think that's what you emptied into me at all."

"Why not?"

"Because I feel braver now," she said, pulling up her underpants and then pulling down her dress. She stood up and slipped her arms around his neck and said, "I feel stronger with your seed inside of me, Hoot. Stronger than I've felt in years."

"That's crazy talk."

"I know, but it's how I feel."

"Shirley, you'd better go right back to Three Rivers," he heard himself tell her. "Did they burn my house?"

"Yes."

"When I come down, we'll go someplace new and start all over again."

"Why?"

Hoot took her back in his arms. "I just don't ever want to see or hear a man that's made love to you for money. I want us to start over—clean and fresh."

Shirley nodded with understanding. "We can go anyplace you like, Hoot. It doesn't matter to me. There is one thing, though."

"What?"

"I want children. I want *your* children."

Hoot nodded, not trusting his voice. He kissed her again as darkness blanketed the mountains. "It's too dark for you to go back now on that steep trail. We'll make camp over there under the trees tonight, and in the morning you'll ride back down to Three Rivers."

Shirley nodded, and although she tried to sound happy, fear was already creeping into her heart and it showed when she said, "Please don't let them kill you, Hoot. I brought you a gun and a rifle."

"Thanks," he said, greatly relieved. "Now I got too much to live for to let myself be killed."

Shirley kissed him again, and then, before the sunlight was all gone, they hurried to make camp and more love.

★

Chapter 17

"What do you make of 'er?" Eli asked the next morning.

Abe scratched the side of his jaw with a torn, dirt-crusted fingernail. "I don't rightly know," he said, peering through the trees at the lone woman on horseback riding down the mountainside.

"Reckon we ought to go find out what she's up to?"

"Reckon so," Abe said, kicking his horse forward.

The woman was still a good half mile away, but she saw the two Hogan brothers almost the instant that they appeared from the cover of the forest. At the sight of them, her face paled and her head whipped around to stare up her backtrail. She seemed caught in a moment of indecision before she stiffened, then squared her shoulders and came riding down the steep, narrow trail.

Abe blocked her path. He grinned, eyes drinking in her full body. "Mornin', ma'am!"

"Good morning," she said without warmth, starting to rein her exhausted horse around the two giants.

But Eli grabbed her bridle. "Hold there, ma'am. Ain't neighborly to just ride on by without a friendly word or two."

"Let go of my horse!"

"Uh-uh," Eli said, his smile fading. "You got to answer a few questions first."

"I don't *have* to do anything!" she snapped, jerking on her reins but finding she was helpless. "Let go!"

Abe rode up on the other side, and his big arm scooped her out of the saddle as easily as if she were a child.

"Let me down!" Shirley screamed, clawing at his face.

"Ouch!" he yelped, dropping her to the ground.

Shirley fell hard, and when she came to her feet to run, she saw that the two big men had both dismounted and that she was sandwiched between them. They scared the hell out of her, but she knew that if she showed fear, she was finished.

"How dare you do this to me!" she cried. "Get out of my way this instant and let me back on my horse or . . ."

"Or what?" Abe asked with a sneer. "You got a man somewhere that'll teach Eli and me some fancy manners?"

"I'll see that you are arrested!"

They laughed at her—put their big hands on their hips and laughed outright. She tried to bolt between them, but they grabbed her, and this time they threw her to the earth.

Shirley's courage melted like the spring snow. She began to shake as she stared up at them, seeing the naked hunger and cruelty in their eyes.

"Please," she begged, "don't hurt me."

Abe squatted down beside her. "We don't want to hurt you, ma'am," he said with exaggerated sincerity. "Do we, Eli?"

"Hell, no!"

"Then let me go. Please."

"We will," Abe said, reaching out to place his hand on her breast. "But first, we need some answers."

She shivered, wanted to scoot away, but Eli was just behind her and there was nothing she could do other than nod her head. "What kind of answers?"

"We want to know where you been up on that mountain and who you seen."

"I . . . I saw my husband," she blurted. "He's a prospector! I was taking him food."

Eli squatted down, and his hand moved under her dress. "I'll bet that isn't all you were bringin' him, huh, pretty lady?"

"Please leave me alone!"

Abe said, "This husband of yours, he find any gold?"

Shirley's mind raced. If she told them yes, she was afraid that they might follow her trail up with the intention of killing her fictional husband for his gold. They'd find Hoot's trail and follow it. But if she said no, they might decide to make sport with her.

"No," she said, her voice filled with bitterness and resignation, "he hasn't."

Eli pushed her dress up above her thighs. "Might be you could give us a little bit of what you gave your husband, eh?"

When she said nothing, Eli looked to his brother and said, "You took that young gal with the wagon first, this one is mine first."

"Fair is fair," Abe grunted, his eyes glazed with lust. "I bet she was just getting herself screwed by some old goat up here, anyways. I bet she ain't even got no husband. Ain't wearing no wedding ring. Bet she ain't nothin' but a little old whore anyhow."

Shirley's mouth was so dry she couldn't speak or even move. She just lay there frozen with fear and dread as Eli unbuckled his pants. She closed her eyes and ground her teeth together when he butted her legs apart and took her like a stud horse taking one of his mares. She listened as he grunted and snorted, and she could hear his brother's hard breathing.

It was the most violent and unpleasant coupling she'd ever endured, but mercifully, it was also very quick. When it was over, the other one got on, and he was just as brutal and punishing. He took longer, but when it was done, he climbed right off.

"What you cryin' for!" he demanded. "Didn't you like it?"

"Can I go now!"

"Yeah, git out of here!" he spat. "You wasn't much of a woman anyhow. No better than screwin' a damned knothole."

Shirley pulled down her dress and stumbled over to her horse. Somehow, she hauled herself into the saddle and whipped her mare on down the trail, hearing them whoop with scornful laughter.

When she was gone, Abe stuffed his manhood back into his pants and said, "I think we ought to go up and see if she was telling the truth. Maybe her man has found some gold."

"Yeah," Eli said.

"And maybe she was the doc's woman and her tracks will lead us straight to him and the Lane brothers."

Eli took a chew of tobacco from his shirt pocket. "Either way," he said, "she felt good."

"Yeah," Abe said agreeably as he scratched his privates and then mounted his horse. "She was just fine."

Two hours later, they came upon the little campground where Hoot and Shirley had spent the night. Abe studied the tracks, and then he and Eli turned to face upslope and off to the south. "That's where he went."

"Then we might as well get goin'," Abe said. "Maybe we'll get real lucky before dark."

Eli nodded. "I kinda wished that I'd used that woman a second time. Would have if we hadn't been in such an all-fired rush."

"Hell," Abe scoffed, "if I was as quick as you were, I'd have wanted seconds, too."

"Go to hell," Eli growled as he mounted his horse and started off on Hoot Anderson's trail.

★

Chapter 18

"If memory serves me correctly," Jessie said, peering through the side curtains of the carriage she'd rented, "this little town is called Three Rivers. We'll stop over here for the night and see if anyone has heard of the Hogan brothers or their captives."

"Why wouldn't they have?" Doc Evans asked. "It's on the way to Santa Fe."

Jessie looked sideways at the young doctor and, riding beside him, Nancy. The woman had washed and brushed her hair. Since they were about the same size, Jessie had given her several dresses to wear, and now she looked quite lovely—a fact that had certainly not escaped the young doctor's eye.

Jessie looked at Evans and said, "It's probable that they did stop here for supplies. But it's also possible that they detoured Three Rivers."

The doctor nodded with understanding, and when their carriage rolled into the little town, they could see that there had just been a very destructive fire.

"Looks like it almost swept the entire town," the doctor said.

Jessie pointed to the ashes of what appeared to have been a blacksmith's shop. "You'll notice that every building in this town is constructed of wood, rather than brick or stone. And these little volunteer fire departments, though well intentioned, are primarily drinking clubs."

"Well," Evans said, "at least they did save the hotel, a few cards and one saloon."

When the samurai drew the coach up in front of the hotel, they were all more than happy to get out and stretch their cramped legs. In less than a quarter hour, Jessie had a separate room and bath for everyone. Ki and Jessie did not waste any time before making inquiries about the Hogan brothers.

"Hogan? Is that really their names?" the hotel desk clerk snapped. "Well I'll tell you one thing, if anyone in Three Rivers ever sees them again it had better be in hell!"

"What is that supposed to mean?" Jessie asked the angry clerk.

"It means them bastards torched Three Rivers!" the man said and choked. "It means that—in one night—they almost destroyed this place and slit our blacksmith's throat!"

"But why?"

"Damned if I know," the clerk said. "No one has quite got the story to where it makes any sense. Doc Anderson is missing and so are three men that was bound ankle and wrist with shackles and chains. Like everyone else, of course, I have my own personal theory."

"And that is?"

"I think that the whole bunch of them was some Colorado gang that got shot up trying to rob a bank up north. So they was on the run, but three of 'em had been arrested and put in chains. Anyway, they got the blacksmith to break them

134

chains and they forced Doc to fix 'em up. After that, it's simple enough to see they killed the blacksmith and took the doc along to keep the wounded alive."

"That's quite a theory," Jessie said. "Any grounds for it?"

"Grounds?" The desk clerk scowled. "What else makes sense? The blacksmith is dead and they found the shackles and chains in the ashes of his shop."

Jessie glanced quickly to one side, at the samurai. The fact that the Lane brothers were no longer shackled was an important piece of information. "And no one has gone after them?"

"Are you asking me if there is any law in Three Rivers?"

"Well, I should think someone here would have at least formed a posse," Jessie said. "After all, they murdered your blacksmith and nearly destroyed your town."

The clerk shook his head with disgust. "Oh, there was a lot of big talk at first. Always is. Then, after everyone sobered up and the steam run out of 'em, they sorta just drifted away and said good riddance."

Jessie's brow knitted with disapproval. "And they didn't even try to rescue their own town doctor?"

"Nope."

Jessie was disgusted. "I don't understand that! In Texas, where I live, if someone rode into a town and did what the Hogan brothers did to Three Rivers, they'd be hunted by every able-bodied man in the county. They'd be caught and hung from the nearest tree."

"I know," the clerk said, "and don't think there aren't any number of us that are ashamed at the fact that nothing was done."

Jessie left the desk clerk, knowing that it would do no good to humiliate him. That evening, when they all got together again for supper, she said, "We have to decide what we need to do next."

"What do you mean?" Nancy asked. "I thought that we were going to Santa Fe."

"You are," Jessie said, "unless you've changed your mind."

"Not at all," Nancy said in a firm voice, "but . . ."

"Listen," Jessie said, addressing them all, "it's clear that the Hogan brothers have gone to find their escaped prisoners. The poor blacksmith removed their chains and died for his kindness. The town doctor got involved too, and now he's missing."

"Probably dead," Evans said quietly.

"Yes," Jessie said, "that's a sad possibility. At any rate, some of us need to investigate."

"What does that mean?" the doctor asked pointedly.

"It means that Ki and I will buy horses and scout this area for a few days while you and Nancy will continue on down to Santa Fe."

"But—"

Jessie cut off his protest. "I promise that we will rejoin you in Santa Fe. But first, Ki and I *have* to find out what happened here."

"But the Hogan brothers might be only a few miles away!" Evans argued. "If that's the case, you'll need our help."

Jessie knew that it was important to be tactful and even flattering. In truth, the doctor and Nancy were a liability if bullets started flying! That's why she had decided that they should continue on to Santa Fe.

"Listen," Jessie said. "We're going to need help in Santa Fe. Perhaps you can convince a United States marshal down there to help us out. And while you're at it, investigate! Find out what is at the bottom of this blood feud between the

Hogans and the Lanes."

"Land," Evans said morosely. "We already know that."

"Yes, but there is much that we don't know and that will be vital if we are to save those brothers.

"What if they are already in Santa Fe?"

"Then," Jessie said quietly, "I hope that you see them before they see you. If that happens, hide until we arrive. It will only be a day—two at the most."

"We'll be fine," the doctor said. "So when do we go our separate ways?"

Jessie looked to Ki. He was almost healed now, and she knew that he was fit enough to endure the rigors and danger they were about to face. "If we can buy horses, we'll be gone before first light tomorrow morning."

Evans nodded. He started to say something, but Jessie was already coming to her feet and bidding them all good night.

That night, Jessie was awakened by a soft knocking at her door. She grabbed her pistol and moved over to the door. "Who is it?"

"It's me, Edward."

"Go away."

"But I need to talk to you, Jessie!"

She opened the door and he stepped inside, then took her in his arms. "Why are you sending me off with that young woman?"

Jessie gently but firmly pushed him back. "Because she needs you," Jessie said.

"And you don't?"

Jessie smiled, and it took the sting out of her words. "No, I don't."

He swallowed. "Then this is it?"

"Uh-huh."

He reached out and touched her breast under the satin

137

pajamas she wore. "What about a little good-bye party?"

"No," she told him. "It's late and I'm half-asleep. Ki and I are—"

Jessie didn't have time to finish explaining, because he took her into his arms and his lips silenced her words. And as his hands moved up and down her body, Jessie's resistance faded and she wrapped her arms around his neck. He picked her up and carried her to his bed.

"You won't be half-asleep when I'm finished with you," he said, voice hoarse with passion as he began to undress.

"No," Jessie said with a catlike smile as she unbuttoned the top of her pajamas to reveal her lush breasts, "I'm sure I won't."

★

Chapter 19

In heavy forest just to the east of Crazy Luke's cabin, Abe dismounted and handed his reins to Eli, saying, "Just stay back here in the trees while I take a look-see."

"It's *got* to be them," Eli said. "The doc and the brothers. Ain't no doubt in my mind it's them."

"If it is," Abe said, pulling his rifle from its saddle boot, "I'll signal you to come along and we'll get the drop on the whole damn bunch."

"I want the pleasure of killin' that doc myself," Eli snarled. "He's caused us a heap of trouble."

Abe agreed, but his mind was too absorbed with getting into position to be thinking about revenge. He needed to get much closer to the log cabin and then wait until someone stepped outside. With that objective in mind, Abe began to dart from tree to tree as he advanced on the cabin. When he was within fifty yards, he sat down, against a big pine tree that shielded him from sight, and checked his weapons.

His rifle, a Winchester repeater, was clean and ready for action, as was his Colt revolver. Abe removed his hat and sleeved sweat from his brow. He twisted around and took a quick peek at the cabin. He could see smoke trickling out of the fireplace. That, coupled with the fact that there was a corral full of horses, made it obvious that there were men inside.

Abe closed his eyes for a moment and wished he were back home at the ranch with his family. Being gone so long with Eli had been trying his nerves. Well, he thought, if they could bag them now, then they would be home in a few more days and everything would be settled. Pa would get the Lane brothers to sign over their ranch and then they'd have a little "hunting accident" up in the mountains and never be heard from again. Either that, or their friendly sheriff would haul them before their even friendlier circuit judge, who would sentence all three to hang for murders that they had not committed.

Either way, Abe thought with a smile, the Lane Ranch would soon belong to their family. It had better land, timber and water than the Hogan Ranch, and it had taken years of whittling the opposition down to get finally to this point. Abe figured that the two ranches becoming one would make his family one of the wealthiest and most powerful in all of the northern New Mexico Territory.

Abe let his mind wander a little as he thought about how good it would be to settle down, maybe take one of the pretty Lane women to wife and then breed her a batch of children. Boys, he hoped, that would take on the work of cattle ranching themselves when he got a little older and stiffer in the joints and decided, like Pa, that it was time to ride a rocking chair instead of a bronc.

It was such a peaceful image that Abe drifted off to sleep and did not awaken until the sound of laughter jerked him out of his reverie.

"Damn fool!" Eli hissed as he came scooting up next to

his brother. "I been tryin' to wake you up for the last ten minutes. It's them!"

Abe twisted around. He saw Doc Anderson and a tall old mountain man sitting on a fallen log next to Orin and Jeb Lane.

"Nate must have cashed it in," Abe said. "He was as good as dead when we reached Three Rivers."

"How we gonna get 'em?" Eli asked. "We need to take Orin and Jeb alive."

"I know that!" Abe snapped. He shot a quick glance around the tree again. "They ain't even armed."

"But the mountain man is," Eli said, "and so's the doc."

"The doc don't worry me none," Abe said. "I'd say the one we got to be careful of is the old man. I've seen enough of his kind to know that most of them can shoot the eyeballs out of a squirrel at a hundred paces."

"So I'll just put a rifle bullet though him and you shoot the doc," Eli said. "Then we'll throw down on Orin and Jeb. If they go for the loose weapons, we can wing 'em."

Abe thought about the plan very carefully. It was, as he'd have expected from his younger brother, simplistic. However, in Abe's experience, simple plans were the best ones. It made good sense to just shoot the mountain man and the doctor. They weren't useful for any good purpose.

"Well?" Eli demanded impatiently.

"All right," Abe said, putting his rifle to his shoulder. "At the count of three we step out on the opposite sides of this pine tree, take aim and on the count of five, we fire. You take the doc; I'll take the old mountain man."

"Sounds good," Eli said.

They stood back to back, rifle barrels pointed straight up. Abe began the count. "One. Two. Three."

On three, they both stepped out from behind the broad trunk of the pine and snapped their rifles to their shoulders.

"Four." Abe drew a head on the mountain man. "Five!"

He squeezed the trigger and had the satisfaction of seeing the old man's buckskin shirt sprout a red blossom. The man went crashing over backward, and Abe knew he was dead before he hit the earth with a bullet through his heart.

At the same time, he saw the doctor spin completely around as Eli's bullet winged his arm. Eli cursed and fired again, but the doctor had been knocked over the log and was shielded from view. And as quick as quail, Orin and Jeb had also thrown themselves behind the log.

"Son of a bitch!" Eli screamed, leaping back behind the tree as the doc poked his head and a six-gun over the log and returned fire.

Abe was furious. "Now we've got a fight on our hands, damn you! Now we are in for it! There's three of them and just two of us!"

Eli levered another shell into the breech of his Winchester. "Yeah, well I suppose you never missed a shot in your life. The goddamn doctor moved just as I opened fire! It was bad luck on my side or I'd have drilled him dead center!"

Abe knew better than to argue with his brother at a time like this. "We got them pinned down," he said. "What we need to do is flank 'em so we can get clear shots in behind that log. If they try and reach the cabin, we can pick them off on the run."

"Yeah," Eli said. "You gonna move first, or am I?"

"I made my shot," Abe said, "you go first."

"Figures," Eli groused, but he took off running low and hard. He was very, very fast on his feet, but he was a large target, and they might have downed him if Abe had not emptied his Colt and kept their heads down below the bark of the log that they were hiding behind.

Eli signaled when he was in covering position, and Abe knew that it was his turn to move off to flank on the right.

Rifle in one fist, gun in the other, he took off, running low and hard. He could hear Eli's covering fire, and when he finally came to a rest, Abe was winded, but not a single bullet had even come close.

"Once more," Abe shouted even as Eli jumped and ran. Abe fired three quick rounds and then Eli was diving for cover. Abe grinned. They were almost in position. If he could get one more good sprint to his right, then he might have a clear line of fire in behind the log.

Abe ducked his head and started running. Again, he heard the fire, but he kept moving as hard as he could. He was almost to the tree he'd selected to hide behind when, suddenly, his left leg went numb, and the next thing he knew he was rolling, ass end up and over. He crashed into the tree, with bullets eating the bark off it, then clawed in behind the trunk, dragging his leg and cussing.

"You all right?" Eli shouted through the trees. "You hit?"

"I'm hit!" Abe shouted, tearing his bandanna from around his neck and using it as a tourniquet. The blood was pumping from his leg, and he knew that the bullet must have hit an artery. Damn the luck! Abe tightened the bandanna until the flow of blood ebbed. Cold sweat beaded on his forehead. He listened to the firing and knew that he was in grave jeopardy. A man could not keep a tourniquet tight around his leg for very long, or he'd soon be killing off his limb and contracting gangrene.

"Abe! Abe, what shall I do?" Eli called.

Abe swallowed. "Keep 'em pinned down!"

More shots answered him, and then Abe shouted, "Don't kill the doc yet!"

"What the—All right!"

Eli yelled at the cabin. "Doc, if you, Orin and Jeb surrender, I swear I won't kill you."

"Go to hell!" Doc yelled.

"My brother is hit!" Eli called. "You help him, you can go free!"

"Sure!" the doctor shouted in a mocking voice. Then he added, "If you want me, come and get me, Eli! Come and get all three of us!"

Abe clutched his leg and twisted around to see Eli gather himself to charge the log. "No!"

Eli twisted around. "Why not!"

"Just . . . just stay put!" Abe shouted. "I'm going to move around. We'll finish 'em off after dark."

"Okay," Eli shouted back.

Abe closed his eyes for a moment. The numbness he'd felt when he was hit was now gone, and in its place, there was a dull, aching throb in his leg. Abe had been shot twice before but never this seriously. He stared at his blood-soaked pant leg and wondered if he would die. Men often did, of far less serious gunshots than this. Usually, a leg wound became infected just as Nate Lane's shoulder wound had become infected. After that happened, death was almost inevitable.

"Doc Anderson!" Abe called. "If you help me, maybe we can strike a deal. Maybe you can have the biggest payday of your life!"

"Not a chance!"

"Doc! I *need* help!"

Abe heard the doctor bark a laugh, and he cried, "You took an oath, Doc! You swore to help a man that was hurt!"

"You aren't a man!" Doc shouted. "You're an animal!"

Abe twisted around and emptied three shots in the general direction of the cabin. His shots were answered, and when the sound of gunfire died, Abe screamed, "We're coming for you, Doc! We're going to kill all of you!"

144

Abe leaned his head back against the bark of the pine tree and closed his eyes. Things were not going well. They were outnumbered and he was in a bad fix. Come the darkness, he and Eli would need a little luck in order to take Orin, Jeb and the doc alive. But if they had no luck—Abe was prepared and very determined to kill all three and Zebulon be damned. He might return to Santa Fe without the Lane brothers, but at least he'd do so knowing that they were dead.

When the sun finally did slide over the highest peaks of the Rockies, Abe began to squirm forward, moving steadily to his right. It was hard and painful, but he knew that he only had to go about twenty yards and then he'd have a clear line of fire. Fortunately, there was a full moon overhead and the visibility was excellent.

It took him almost ten minutes to get in position behind a rock. Abe eased his head up, and then a curse escaped his lips because the three men were gone. Abe dropped below his cover and ground his teeth against the pain in his leg. Things were not going well at all.

He was about to call out to Eli when, suddenly, a volley of gunfire erupted in that general direction. It lasted only a minute or two but seemed much longer. And when the last report died, Abe shouted, "Eli!"

Seconds passed. Abe's heart raced, and then he heard a cry of pain and a scream.

"Eli!"

"I got 'em!" Eli shouted triumphantly. "I got the doc and Orin!"

"What about Jeb?"

"I killed him!"

Abe expelled a deep sigh of relief. "Bring the doc over here with his medicine bag and a lantern!" Abe called weakly. "And . . . and good work!"

★

Chapter 20

Hoot did not rise to his feet even when Eli kicked him in the side. Instead, he made sure that the last flutter of life was gone from young Jeb Lane.

"He was a fine young man," Hoot said, looking up at Eli.

"He was a fool and if you don't stand up and help my brother, I'll kill you and Orin—right now."

"No, you won't," Hoot said, surprised at how calm he felt inside. "Because you still need us. Without me, your brother will surely die. Without Orin, you've failed completely. Won't have a signature for that ranch land you plan to steal. That's why—unless you are a complete idiot—you won't kill either one of us."

"Stand up!" Eli screamed, cocking back the hammer of his gun. "Stand up or say hello, hell!"

Hoot sighed and stood. "It's dark out there," he said wearily. "We'll need that lantern burning inside the cabin."

"Let's get it then," Eli said. He motioned them both toward the cabin with the barrel of his six-gun. "Orin, you lay down—face first by the door where I can keep an eye on you. Doc, you go inside and grab the lantern and your medical kit. Just remember, one false move and I'll shoot you both."

Hoot went inside and Orin followed him. Suddenly, Eli saw Nate resting on a cot. He was lying on his side, face to the wall.

"He's dead, ain't he?"

"Yeah," Hoot lied. "He passed on just a little while ago. We were going to bury him first thing in the morning."

Eli walked over to Nate. He grabbed his shoulder. "Why, he ain't even stiff yet!"

"Like I said, he just—"

Eli wasn't listening. He grabbed Nate's wrist, and when he felt a fluttering pulse, his eyes widened. "Why, he's still alive! I don't need him anymore," Eli crowed, cocking back the hammer of his six-gun.

Hoot had grabbed their kerosene lantern, and now he hurled it across the interior of the cabin. The lantern struck Eli in the face. Eli screamed as kerosene drenched his beard and upper body. A split second later, the lantern exploded in flame and Eli's beard ignited like a pitch torch.

It was both horrible and fascinating to watch as Eli dropped his gun and beat at his fiery face and chest. Hoot recoiled as Eli's agonizing screams filled the interior of the cabin. He watched as Eli slammed out through the open doorway to reel around the yard, hollering like something gone mad, as the fire burned away his facial features.

Hoot staggered to the door, intent on grabbing a gun and putting the man out of his misery. Orin beat him to it. He snatched up Crazy Luke's rifle, then threw it to his shoulder and fired. Hoot saw Eli stagger, and the scream died in his throat.

Orin fired again, and Eli crumpled to his knees, still trying to beat at what was left of his charred face. Now,

147

Orin held his fire, and Hoot was shocked to see that he was grinning.

"Finish him!" Hoot shouted. "Put him out of his misery!"

Orin shook his head and watched as Eli batted feebly at his burning face.

"Kill him!" Hoot shouted, jumping forward to grab the pistol that Shirley had given him.

"No!" Orin cried. "Let him—"

Whatever Orin was going to say ended suddenly as Abe's rifle bullet struck him between the eyes. Orin threw his arms to the sky, then pitched over backward in death. A second shot mercifully blew the back of Eli's skull away. A moment later Abe hobbled into the yard.

"Now," Abe shouted, "it's just you and me and you're going to dig this slug out of my leg before I bleed to death."

Hoot shook his head. "I don't believe that I will. I'd rather die now than save you only to die later."

"You help me," Abe panted, hobbling closer, "and I *swear* I'll spare your life."

"Do you really expect me to believe that?"

"Then believe this," Abe said, raising his Winchester. "As long as there is life, there is hope. Doc, I'll give you just five seconds to make up your mind—life or death."

Hoot used every one of his five seconds, and when they were up, he knew that Abe was right. He cursed his own fear and weakness, but he did want to live. The idea of never making love to Shirley again, after spending his entire life searching for a woman like that, filled him with an overpowering sadness.

"All right," he whispered, turning back toward the cabin. "Come on inside and I'll see what I can do."

Abe hobbled after him. Hoot found a candle and lit it, then motioned for Abe to take a chair. Abe started to, but

148

then, like his brother, his eyes fell on Nate.

"He's alive?"

Hoot knew better than to lie a second time. "Yeah."

Abe grinned. "Then we *didn't* fail! Not as long as one of them is alive to deed their ranch over to my pa."

"Nate is in bad shape."

"He'll live," Abe said with conviction. "Lane men are easier to shoot than to kill. Now, take a look at my leg."

"Sit down."

Abe sat, but he did not take his gun out of Hoot's face. "Well?"

"I'll have to dig out the slug. It's going to be rough."

"Life is rough. Get it out!"

"You could bleed to death while I'm digging around inside for the slug."

"Before that happens," Abe vowed, "I'll use my last breath to kill you and Nate."

"I know that," Hoot said, going to his medical kit and getting his forceps, sutures and bandaging.

It took him fifteen minutes to dig the slug out of Abe's muscular thigh and another ten minutes to clean and bandage the wound. Anyone with less than the constitution of a horse would have expired, or at least fainted.

"What now?" Abe asked weakly.

"Rest. You can't move the leg until it scabs over. Otherwise, the bleeding might start again. You've already lost too much blood."

"We are leaving in the morning," Abe said, "bad leg or no bad leg."

"But—"

"I'll show you how to make us a couple of travois," Abe explained. "One for Nate, the other for me. We got plenty of horses in the corral. In two days at the most, I'll be home."

"You'll never make it."

"If I don't," Abe vowed, "neither will you."

Hoot believed the man. He also believed that Abe probably would survive the hard trip over the mountains to Santa Fe. As for Nate, well, that was another matter. Nate was still fighting a fever brought on by the infection. With Nate, it would be touch and go for another week or two. After that—if he were still alive—Hoot liked the man's chances.

In the morning, just at daybreak, Hoot was jarred into wakefulness by Abe. "Get up! We got a lot to do before we pull out of here."

Hoot was soon to learn what Abe meant. First, he was ordered to cut a staff for Abe to lean on while the wounded giant hobbled about giving instructions on how to make three travois instead of just two—one for himself, another for Nate, and the third for all the supplies they would carry on to Santa Fe.

"I don't mean to leave a damn thing of value if it can be brought along," Abe grunted.

Hoot had no difficulty fashioning the travois, and then, with Abe's instructions, he was able to get them mounted to the horses. By the time everything was loaded and lashed down tightly, it was early afternoon.

"I guess we are ready," Hoot said, when Abe eased down upon the travois.

"Not quite." Abe motioned his gun barrel toward the bodies of Crazy Luke, Jeb, Orin and the horrible remains of his own brother. "Drag 'em into the cabin and set it afire."

"What!"

"You heard me! Otherwise, the animals will just eat 'em!"

"I could take an hour or two and bury 'em."

"No time for that," Abe said. "Get 'em inside and put a match to it."

Hoot could see that Abe's mind was made up and that it could not be changed, so he dragged Crazy Luke into the cabin and laid him out in the middle of the floor. "I'm sorry I got you into this," he said to the still body. "It was none of your doing."

Next he grabbed Jeb and Orin and pulled them into the cabin. "You should have showed mercy to Eli. Maybe if you had, you'd still be alive. I'm sorry."

"All right," Abe said, "drag my brother in there with 'em and light a match. Time is wasted on the dead."

Hoot's years of being Three Rivers' dentist, doctor and mortician had damn near made him immune to death and suffering, but when he stepped over to grab what remained of Eli, he almost vomited. The man's face was burned cheese. His nose was gone, his lips, ears and eyes were gone. Only char and the glistening white bone of cheek and teeth remained.

"Get him in there!" Abe screamed.

Hoot grabbed the giant's wrists, which were covered with running blisters that popped in his grip. Trying hard not to vomit, Hoot pulled and struggled until he had Eli's body inside. Then, he quickly lit a match, touched it to a pile of gunnysacks and the bedding and staggered outside.

The log cabin ignited fast. Before Hoot had even led the horses and their travois across the mountain meadow, the cabin was crackling like a funeral pyre.

Abe watched it burn, his face as hard and brittle as a mask. Looking back at the man, Hoot wondered what the giant was thinking. But on second thought, he decided that he really did not want to know.

★

Chapter 21

Ki ran his hand through the ashes. They were stone cold. Jessie watched him in silence. When he lifted a skull by the hair, she gulped.

"Are there any more victims?"

"Three more," Ki said.

"Any way of telling . . ."

"One was probably a Hogan," Ki said, measuring the huge bones of an arm. "I can't say about the other two."

"The others could be that missing doctor from Three Rivers and one of the Lane brothers," Jessie said. "Or perhaps just two innocent men who happened to be here when the Hogan brothers showed up. At least they seem to have killed one of them before they were themselves slaughtered."

Ki nodded. He stepped out of the ashes, went over to the empty horse corral and studied the tracks.

"I read two travois," Jessie said.

"Yes," Ki answered, "and they're heading in the direction of Santa Fe."

"How far ahead of us?"

"A full day. Maybe a day and a half."

Jessie looked to the southwest. "Then I doubt we shall overtake them before they reach Santa Fe."

"We can try," the samurai said, moving quickly to his horse. He mounted the animal, then rode over to Jessie, who sat her own horse before the burned rubble of the cabin.

"Everywhere those brothers go, they leave ashes," she said. "First at Nancy's wagon where we found her, then at Three Rivers, now here. I wonder which one was killed and how?"

"Does it matter?"

Jessie shook her head. "No, it doesn't," she said. "Let's go."

They rode off at a fast trot and kept that pace all day. Their camp was made in starlight and abandoned in the glow of the rising sun. Full daybreak found them in New Mexico Territory, still following the track of the horses and the travois.

Jessie could see that they were rapidly closing the gap, but it was late afternoon when they crossed over the last rugged range of the Sangre de Cristo Mountains and saw the great bowl where Santa Fe rested and had prospered for centuries as a trading center.

Santa Fe was situated on the banks of the Santa Fe River, a small tributary of the Rio Grande River. It could trace its roots back hundreds of years, but the Spaniards claimed to have founded it in 1610. Jessie knew enough Spanish to realize that the name Santa Fe meant "Holy Faith."

Santa Fe had a violent history. In 1680, the Pueblo Indians, weary of being oppressed by the brutal Spaniards, staged a successful revolt and captured the town after weeks of bloody fighting. Twelve years passed before the Spaniards were able to recapture the ancient pueblo. During the following two centuries, Mexicans, Apache, mountain men and pillagers of every race and description had assaulted and claimed the town. It was not until the Americans took control and the Civil War had passed that the turmoil was finally ended and Old Santa Fe at last became a peaceful trading center.

Jessie and Ki had no sooner arrived at the old plaza when they heard a shout and saw Dr. Edward Evans and Nancy come hurrying over to greet them. Edward hugged Jessie and pumped Ki's hand. "We were worried about you. What did you find up in the Rockies?"

Jessie's smile died. Quickly, she told the couple about discovering the charred remains of three men in the ruins of a cabin fire.

"And you don't know who they could be?" Nancy asked, her blue eyes troubled.

"Ki measured the length of a bone and feels certain that one of the bodies belonged to a giant, probably one of the Hogan brothers. As for the other two . . . well, there is just no way of knowing."

Edward put his arm around Nancy's shoulders, and Jessie saw an intimacy pass between them. Edward said, "Nancy's memory has returned almost completely. She believes that she can identify the men who killed her family."

"Good," Jessie said. "Have you had time to find out anything about the trouble between the Lane and Hogan families?"

"You bet we have," Edward said. "It's a bloody feud that spans about thirty years. At one time, both clans were pretty equally matched. But over the last five or six years, the Hogan brothers have all but wiped out the Lane men. They've ambushed them one by one."

"The four that were left were the last of the lot," Nancy said. "Everyone knew they were running for their lives and that Abe and Eli Hogan went hunting for them after bragging all over town that they'd track them down."

"What about that business of them being deputized by some judge?" Jessie asked.

"There's nothing to that at all," Edward said. "As far as their badges, well, it's common knowledge that they own the town marshal. They probably just got him to deputize them in exchange for a little cash."

Jessie glanced at Ki. "I think we need to pay a visit to the Lane Ranch and hear what they have to say before we take on the Hogan family."

"This time," Edward said firmly, "Nancy and I want to come along."

"All right," Jessie said. "First thing tomorrow morning, we'll ride out to the Lane Ranch and tell them that their boys are either all dead or else badly injured."

"We only know that one is dead for certain," Ki said. "The first one that was killed on the Central Pacific Railroad crossing over Donner Pass."

"I know," Jessie said, "but it would be a miracle if the other three were still alive."

Ki agreed. Jessie was right and, from what he'd seen, the poor Lane brothers had run out of miracles the day they were tracked down and captured in California.

★

Chapter 22

They had no difficulty finding the Lane Ranch, or what remained of it after years of drought, feuding and destruction. The ranch house itself was a large, crumbling adobe structure. There were quite a few outbuildings, also constructed of adobe, including a blacksmith shop, several storage sheds and a barn with a cracked tile roof. It was easy to see that Lane Ranch had once been a pretty nice-looking operation, but that had been many years in the past.

"Do you get the feeling," Ki asked, as they rode into a ranch yard deserted except for a few goats, dogs and chickens, "that we are all resting squarely in someone's gun sights?"

"Yes, they're pointed at us from the house, the barn and the blacksmith shop, as well as that storage shed to our right," Jessie said, keeping her eyes straight ahead.

"Hello the house!" Jessie yelled when they came to the front porch and no one appeared to greet them. "Anybody home?"

They waited almost a full minute before an old man in bib

overalls appeared with a double-barreled shotgun clenched in his liver-spotted hands. He was shirtless and hatless and did not look well.

"Who are ya!" he demanded.

"My name is Jessica Starbuck. This is Mrs. Nancy Spicer and that is Dr. Edward Evans."

"Who is that Chinaman?"

"I'm not a Chinaman," Ki said. "My name is Ki and I'm half-American, half-Japanese."

"Humph!" the old man said, keeping his shotgun trained on them. "What do you want?"

"It's about your sons," Jessie said. "I'm afraid that John is dead. He was shot by the Hogan brothers while trying to escape from a train passing over the Sierra Nevada Mountains."

The old man blinked. "John is dead?"

"Yes," Jessie said. "I'm sorry. He and his brothers were captured on the Feather River. Abe and Eli told everyone that they were wanted for murder in Santa Fe. We've since found out that that isn't true."

The old man lowered his shotgun. "They was all good boys. I'm the one sent 'em off. I deeded this land over to the four of 'em and told them to skedaddle for a few years. I was hopin' . . . Well, Miss, I don't know what I was hopin'. But I just knowed they'd all have been killed just like all the other menfolk 'cept me and a couple of the boys."

"Are the boys the ones that have us in their gun sights?" Jessie asked.

"They are."

"We mean you no harm," Jessie said. "In fact, we've done all that we can to help your boys. I'm afraid that we weren't very successful. I can't say for certain, but they all might be dead."

The old man paled. He staggered and might even have fallen if Edward and Ki had not escorted him over to a rocking chair.

"Sit and rest," Ki said. "We're not certain if they are all dead or not. I am quite sure that at least one of the Hogan brothers—Eli or Abe—is dead. We found his charred remains in a fire up in the mountains."

"Good!" the old man hissed, clenching his fists as tears washed down his sunken cheeks.

A few minutes passed, and then the rest of the Lane family began to appear. They were all girls, old women or boys. There were no men except the one sitting and weeping silently in his rocking chair.

One of the women, who appeared to be about forty, went inside and reappeared a few minutes later with glasses of goat's milk and cookies. "Couldn't help hearin' you say that my sons are all dead," the woman told Ki.

"We're not sure," he replied.

"But you think so?"

"I don't know. We're expecting whoever's left to show up in Santa Fe or at the Hogan Ranch today."

The woman turned on the old man and her fact twisted with fury. "Quit your damn blubberin'! We need to go kill the Hogans! And I don't care if we all die tryin'! We should never have sent the boys away. It got 'em killed and it was your idea, Grandpa!"

The old man began to sob even louder, and Jessie turned away, feeling pity. She didn't know all the circumstances behind this tragic feud, but it was plain to see that this family was almost wiped out and that Grandpa Lane had made an unfortunate decision. Sometimes that happened, and Jessie did not see where haranguing the poor old man would make things any better.

"We're going to leave right away," she said, "and we mean to get to the bottom of this. Mrs. Spicer's husband and parents were set upon and murdered just north of Denver, probably by Abe and Eli. If she can identify them, then we'll see that justice is done."

"You'll just get yourself raped and then shot," the woman said. "Don't you have any sense! Them big men are killers! They'll show you no mercy."

The woman's voice dropped to a hush. "I'm . . . I'm sorry, Miss. But you're talkin' foolishness if you and your friends think you can just ride onto the Hogan Ranch and arrest them menfolks. They'll kill the Chinaman and your tall young friend, and then they'll have sport with you and this poor widow woman."

Jessie glanced at Nancy and saw how pale she had become. "Nancy, we can take you back to Santa Fe. You too, Edward."

"No," they said in unison. The doctor did something else. He tossed his glass of goat's milk down and then remounted his horse. "I don't see any point in bothering these poor folks in their time of grief, do you, Jessie?"

"No," she said, "I don't."

They remounted and were about to rein their horses away when Jessie paused for a moment. "Where is the Hogan ranch house?"

The woman pointed, her face hard and bitter. "About ten miles yonder. You want a little advice?"

"You've already given us plenty," Jessie said.

"Well, I'll give you a little bit more . . . Go in at night and burn their house down, and when they come out, shoot 'em down to the last man, woman and child! Kill every damned one of them!"

Jessie had never seen such pure hatred in one woman's

159

eyes in her entire life. The sad thing was that she also saw it in the children's eyes.

But then, given the news she'd just brought to this place, how could she have expected otherwise?

★

Chapter 23

By the time that his travois bounced and grated across the Hogan ranch yard, Abe was faint from the loss of blood and his mind was dull from too many long, pain-filled hours. He had managed to keep his gun trained on Hoot the entire journey down from the cabin where his brother's body lay under a carpet of smoking ashes.

Now, as the Hogan cowboys came rushing out and began to ask questions, Abe roused himself and looked into the eyes of his father, Zebulon. The old giant's chiseled face was hard and unsmiling.

"Tell it," he said between clenched teeth.

Abe swallowed. "As you can see, I brought Nate back; the other three of 'em are kilt."

"And Eli? What happened to him?"

"Eli got hisself shot in the mountains above Three Rivers."

Zebulon's eyes tightened around the corners. Eli had always been his favorite. "You let that happen?"

"I couldn't help it, Pa!"

Zebulon turned away and moved over to Hoot, who stood

surrounded by the Hogan clan. They parted when Zebulon demanded, "Who the hell are you?"

"I'm a doctor. I come from Three Rivers."

"He's the cause of us losin' Eli!" Abe swore, raising a hand and pointing an accusing finger at Hoot. "He double-crossed us. Took the Lane brothers up into the mountains to hide. Skin him alive, Pa!"

Zebulon's right hand doubled into a fist, and when he swung, it was from his boot tops. Hoot took the roundhouse blow against his jaw, and lights exploded behind his eyes. He didn't feel Zebulon's boot crash into the sides of his ribs, cracking three of them.

"Boss, you want me to gut him for ya?" one of the Hogan men asked.

"Naw," the old patriarch said, "we're going to need him to help Abe mend right. Take and tie him up in that extra bedroom. Make sure that he can't escape."

Hoot was dragged away, and Zebulon went back to look at Nate. "You damn sure better not die on me, you son of a bitch!"

Nate looked up at the old man who bore the responsibility for the murder of his father, his uncles and his brothers. "There is nothing that you can do to make me sign over the ranch. Nothing!"

Zebulon smiled wickedly. He reached down and pulled Nate's blankets back, then ripped the bandage off his shoulder. "Looks purty bad to me," he said loud enough for everyone to hear. "Looks like we might have to just clean that out a little. Best thing for that is a red hot poker."

Sweat beaded across Nate Lane's body. "I won't sign nothin'!" he cried.

"We'll see," Zebulon said, unholstering his six-gun and bringing it down hard on Nate's shoulder.

"Ahhhh!"

162

The scab was torn off, and the wound reopened and began to bleed. Zebulon chuckled. "Hell, boy, that's like a feather tickle compared to what it'll feel like when I use the poker. Maybe you better change your mind."

Nate was breathing hard, and he thought maybe he'd urinated in his pants.

"You'll sign papers," Zebulon said confidently. "You'll sign 'em one way or the other."

Zebulon turned to his foreman. "Take a couple of the boys and ride for Santa Fe. Have lawyer Deavers draw up a deed of sale for the Lane Ranch. I've given him instructions so he knows exactly what I want put in writing. Bring it back and don't stop in the goddamn saloons!"

"Yes, sir!"

"What about Nate?" one of the cowboys asked. "He's bleedin' from that shoulder. Ain't goin' to do you any good if he dies, Boss."

Zebulon nodded his head. "We'll give him and that Three Rivers doc the night to think on it, then we'll do what needs to be done tomorrow morning. By then I'll have the deed ready for Nate to sign. No sense aggravatin' him until we get the damned thing."

"So where are we going to keep him?"

Zebulon frowned. He watched as his foreman and riders galloped out of the yard, heading for nearby Santa Fe. If lawyer Deavers was still sober this late in the afternoon, he would have the deed drawn up before dark. If the fool lawyer was already drunk, he might have to work half the night. In either case, Zebulon knew that the deed would be ready for Nate's signature tomorrow morning.

"Boss? I said, where—"

"Put him in the same room as the doc," Zebulon said. "And I want two men to stay on guard all night. Work it in three-hour shifts so no one falls asleep."

163

"Yes, sir!"

Zebulon watched as Nate was yanked off his travois and then dragged roughly into the house. To no one in particular, the old man said, "I almost hope that the son of a bitch does try to hold out. Be a lot more fun breaking his mind than just putting a bullet in him. A hell of a lot more fun."

It was just before daybreak the following morning that Zebulon heard the sound of hoofbeats pounding into the yard. He rolled out of bed and went to his window. He could see his foremen and the cowboys he'd sent to Santa Fe dismounting. He noticed that they were visibly staggering, and he knew that they'd been drinking.

To hell with it, he thought. They probably had to wait for hours while Deavers sobered up enough to draft the deed. Zebulon opened his window and bellowed, "Did you get it?"

The foreman wheeled around in a full circle. He looked up, mouth hanging open, face frozen with fear as if he had heard the voice of God coming down from the heavens. "Yes, sir!"

"Then bring it in for me to study, damn you!"

Several minutes later, the man barged into Zebulon's room, full of excuses for his tardiness as he handed over the newly drafted deed.

"Get the hell out of here!" Zebulon ordered. "I told you to stay out of the saloons and you go and get drunk."

"But . . ."

Zebulon grabbed the man and hurled him across the hallway. The foreman slammed into the wall, cracking the back of his head very hard. His knees buckled momentarily, but so great was his fear of Zebulon that it kept him on his feet and he rushed away.

Zebulon took the deed over to his desk. He smoothed it

164

out and read it over once quickly, then a second time very carefully. It was fine. There was money to be paid—which would have been "stolen" by the time that Nate's body was recovered. The "price" was even fair, $12,000, a little less than one dollar an acre. The terms, of course, were cash on signature.

It took Zebulon a full hour to read and reread the document until he was absolutely certain that it would stand up in court. Satisfied, he dressed and went downstairs to breakfast, but not until he'd give orders that both the doctor and Nate should have a last breakfast as well. Zebulon also gave the order that the forge should be fired and a poker heated to a glow.

"We'll just see how long he can last," Zebulon said happily. "My guess is that, unless I kill him by mistake, he won't last ten minutes. Can you read and write?"

"No, sir," the cowboy said.

"It don't matter. I got Nate's signature from an IOU he wrote at the saddlery in town. If he dies, then you can practice copying it until it looks the same."

The cowboy grimly nodded and headed for the blacksmith shop.

★

Chapter 24

On their way to the Hogan Ranch that morning, a cold wind began to blow. And up along the spiral peaks of the Sangre de Cristos, bolts of lightning danced to the rumble of thunder.

"The weather suits the occasion," Edward said dryly. "I think there is a very good chance we might all wind up dead before dark."

"I don't believe that," Jessie said, "and neither should you. But if you feel that way, it's still not too late for you and Nancy to turn your horses around and go back to Santa Fe."

"No, thanks," Edward said. "I've come this far, I won't quit now."

"And I *can't* go back," Nancy said. "If I did, I'd never forgive myself for letting down my dead husband and parents."

Jessie understood, but she was worried. That worry did not diminish but grew more intense when she saw the distant Hogan Ranch buildings. At that same moment, Ki reined his horse off the trail into the trees.

"One hour," he said, "then come on in and I will be waiting and ready."

Jessie nodded and watched as the samurai tied his horse in the trees, then disappeared. "We might as well dismount and stretch our legs," she said, leading her horse into the same stand of trees.

"Do you think he really will get into that house?" Nancy asked.

"Certainly. Not only that, but if either the doctor or any of the Lane brothers are inside, he'll find and protect them."

"What about us?" Edward said.

"He'll try and protect us, too," Jessie said, loosening her cinch.

The next hour passed very slowly and no one said much of anything. Finally, Jessie moved over to her horse and tightened the cinch. "Let's ride in as if this is nothing but a social call."

"A social call?" Edward echoed. "Why, we are likely to be shot out of our saddles!"

"I don't think so," Jessie said, mounting her horse and touching spurs to its flanks.

While still about a quarter mile from the ranch house, Jessie thought she heard a scream, but the wind was blowing hard and she could not be certain. The sound might even have been that of some animal in the forest.

When they walked their horses into the ranch yard a few minutes later, dogs started to bark, and there was a knot of cowboys on the front porch who turned and faced them. The tracks of the three travois led right up to the front porch and Jessie saw poles lying off to the side of the house.

"I'll let you do the talking," Edward gulped nervously as they drew their horses to a standstill.

Jessie studied the ranch hands. They were a hard lot, about what she would have expected to work for the Hogan family.

"What do you want?" one of the older men on the porch demanded.

"I came to see the men that were brought in on those travois."

"What travois?"

"The ones that made those lines on the ground," she said, pointing at the tracks.

The man was about to say something when a blood-curdling cry erupted from inside the house. Jessie's hand flashed for her gun, and she heard a shot from inside.

Before she could throw herself from the saddle, Ki and a huge old man crashed through the front window of the house. They struck the porch, rolled over and over, then landed on the ground.

Jessie had no doubt that she was seeing the elder Hogan. He was massive and still a powerful man, as his huge hands gripped the samurai's throat and tried to throttle the life out of him.

One of the cowboys drew his six-gun, but Jessie's was already out, and she cried, "No! This is their fight!"

Ki's face was turning purple, and he was underneath the rancher, who greatly outweighed and outmuscled him. And just when Jessie was about to take matters into her own hands, the samurai kicked upward, locked his heels around the giant's head and pulled him over backward. The samurai was quicker by far, but when he came to his feet, Zebulon already had a big knife clenched in his fist.

The cowboys grinned and relaxed. It seemed obvious to Jessie that they had seen their boss carve up a man before.

"Jessie?" Edward whispered.

168

"It's all right," she assured the doctor.

Zebulon feinted twice, and when the samurai appeared to be inexperienced and take both feints, the old man kicked out with his left foot, then lunged forward, bringing the sharp edge of his blade slashing upward toward Ki's belly.

The samurai jumped back, and his foot shot out in a sweep lotus that caught the giant just under the chin. Zebulon grunted and staggered. Ki unleashed another kick to the man's gut, which bent him over. Zebulon took a back step, and then his face flushed and he lunged again.

Ki would have easily avoided the onrushing man, but one of the cowboys tripped him. Jessie's heart flew up to her throat as she saw the giant pounce on Ki and try to bury his knife to the hilt. The samurai twisted in a desperate attempt to avoid taking the bigger man's steel, and then he drove his thumbs into Zebulon's eyes.

The rancher bellowed in pain and stabbed furiously, but Ki grabbed his opponent's wrists, and when they rolled, Jessie saw the rancher's mouth fly open. For a moment the big man seemed to scream silently to his men for help; then he collapsed, and when Ki jumped to his feet, everyone saw the knife protruding from the rancher's chest.

"Damn you!"

Jessie's head swung around to see Abe with a gun in his hand as he staggered into the doorway. She fired instinctively, without taking time to aim or even think, fired again and again, until Abe was on his toes and being driven back into the house.

They all heard Abe crash to the hallway floor.

"Freeze!" Jessie yelled, pointing her gun at the stunned cowboys.

To their credit, Edward and Nancy also had their guns out and trained on the stunned ranch hands. "Keep them

169

covered," Jessie ordered, throwing herself from her horse and rushing into the house.

It took her only a moment to find Nate and the doctor from Three Rivers. Nate was no longer bleeding from the shoulder, because his wound had been cauterized by a poker, the searing end of which still smoked with the stench of burned flesh.

"Who are you?" Hoot whispered, his face white with fear. "An angel from heaven?"

Jessie holstered her six-gun. She went over to Nate and looked down into his long-suffering eyes. "It's over," she told the suffering man. "Your brothers are all dead, but so are the Hogan men."

"Am I . . . am I going to live?"

Jessie nodded. "We've two doctors here now. I think that between the two of them, you're going to be just fine. And so is your family."

"What's left of it," he choked.

"Yes," Jessie said, remembering the pitiful few that remained.

She started to go back outside, but Nate grabbed her arm. "Thank you," he said very softly. "Thanks for saving my life."

Jessie saw a flash of lightning and heard the rumble of thunder that followed. "There's a storm moving in over this country. I can feel rain in the air. Maybe it will end the drought and maybe it will wash all the hate and blood away."

"Maybe," Nate said with a hopeful smile, which was enough to tell Jessie that, given rain and a long period of healing, everything was going to be all right.

Watch for

LONE STAR AND THE GUNRUNNERS

121st in the exciting LONE STAR series
from Jove

Coming in September!

Fury knew something was wrong long before he saw the wagon train spread out, unmoving, across the plains in front of him.

From miles away, he had noticed the cloud of dust kicked up by the hooves of the mules and oxen pulling the wagons. Then he had seen that tan-colored pall stop and gradually be blown away by the ceaseless prairie wind.

It was the middle of the afternoon, much too early for a wagon train to be stopping for the day. Now, as Fury topped a small, grass-covered ridge and saw the motionless wagons about half a mile away, he wondered just what kind of damn fool was in charge of the train.

Stopping out in the open without even forming into a circle was like issuing an invitation to the Sioux, the Cheyenne, or the Pawnee. War parties roamed these plains all the time just looking for a situation as tempting as this one.

Fury reined in, leaned forward in his saddle, and thought about it. Nothing said he had to go help those pilgrims. They might not even want his help. But from the looks of things, they needed his help, whether they wanted it or not.

He heeled the rangy lineback dun into a trot toward the wagons. As he approached, he saw figures scurrying back and forth around the canvas-topped vehicles. Looked sort of like an anthill after someone stomped it.

Fury pulled the dun to a stop about twenty feet from the lead wagon. Near it a man was stretched out on the ground with so many men and women gathered around him that Fury could only catch a glimpse of him through the crowd. When some of the men turned to look at him, Fury said, "Howdy. Thought it looked like you were having trouble."

"Damn right, mister," one of the pilgrims snapped. "And if you're of a mind to give us more, I'd advise against it."

Fury crossed his hands on the saddlehorn and shifted in the saddle, easing his tired muscles. "I'm not looking to cause trouble for anybody," he said mildly.

He supposed he might appear a little threatening to a bunch of immigrants who until now had never been any farther west than the Mississippi. Several days had passed since his face had known the touch of the razor, and his rough-hewn features could be a little intimidating even without the beard stubble. Besides that, he was well armed with a Colt's Third Model Dragoon pistol holstered on his right hip, a Bowie knife sheathed on his left, and a Sharps carbine in the saddleboot under his right thigh. And he had the look of a man who knew how to use all three weapons.

A husky, broad-shouldered six-footer, John Fury's height was apparent even on horseback. He wore a broad-brimmed, flat-crowned black hat, a blue work shirt, and fringed buckskin pants that were tucked into high-topped black boots. As he swung down from the saddle, a man's voice, husky with strain, called out, "Who's that? Who are you?"

The crowd parted, and Fury got a better look at the figure on the ground. It was obvious that he was the one who had spoken. There was blood on the man's face, and from the twisted look of him as he lay on the ground, he was busted up badly inside.

Fury let the dun's reins trail on the ground, confident that the horse wouldn't go anywhere. He walked over to the injured man and crouched beside him. "Name's John Fury," he said.

The man's breath hissed between his teeth, whether in pain or surprise Fury couldn't have said. "Fury? I heard of you."

Fury just nodded. Quite a few people reacted that way when they heard his name.

"I'm . . . Leander Crofton. Wagonmaster of . . . this here train." The man struggled to speak. He appeared to be in his fifties and had a short, grizzled beard and the leathery skin of a man who had spent nearly his whole life outdoors. His pale blue eyes were narrowed in a permanent squint.

"What happened to you?" Fury asked.

"It was a terrible accident—" began one of the men standing nearby, but he fell silent when Fury cast a hard glance at him. Fury had asked Crofton, and that was who he looked toward for the answer.

Crofton smiled a little, even though it cost him an effort. "Pulled a damn fool stunt," he said. "Horse nearly stepped on a rattler, and I let it rear up and get away from me. Never figured the critter'd spook so easy." The wagonmaster paused to draw a breath. The air rattled in his throat and chest. "Tossed me off and stomped all over me. Not the first time I been stepped on by a horse, but then a couple of the oxen pullin' the lead wagon got me, too,'fore the driver could get 'em stopped."

"God forgive me, I . . . I am so sorry." The words came in a tortured voice from a small man with dark curly hair and a beard. He was looking down at Crofton with lines of misery etched onto his face.

"Wasn't your fault, Leo," Crofton said. "Just . . . bad luck."

Fury had seen men before who had been trampled by horses. Crofton was in a bad way, and Fury could tell by the look in the man's eyes that Crofton was well aware of it. The wagonmaster's chances were pretty slim.

"Mind if I look you over?" Fury asked. Maybe he could do something to make Crofton's passing a little easier, anyway.

One of the other men spoke before Crofton had a chance to answer. "Are you a doctor, sir?" he asked.

Fury glanced up at him, saw a slender, middle-aged man with iron-gray hair. "No, but I've patched up quite a few hurt men in my time."

"Well, I am a doctor," the gray-haired man said. "And I'd appreciate it if you wouldn't try to move or examine Mr. Crofton. I've already done that, and I've given him some laudanum to ease the pain."

Fury nodded. He had been about to suggest a shot of whiskey, but the laudanum would probably work better.

Crofton's voice was already slower and more drowsy from the drug as he said, "Fury . . ."

"Right here."

"I got to be sure about something . . . You said your name was . . . John Fury."

"That's right."

"The same John Fury who . . . rode with Fremont and Kit Carson?"

"I know them," Fury said simply.

"And had a run-in with Cougar Johnson in Santa Fe?"

"Yes."

"Traded slugs with Hemp Collier in San Antone last year?"

"He started the fight, didn't give me much choice but to finish it."

"Thought so." Crofton's hand lifted and clutched weakly at Fury's sleeve. "You got to . . . make me a promise."

Fury didn't like the sound of that. Promises made to dying men usually led to a hell of a lot of trouble.

Crofton went on, "You got to give me . . . your word . . . that you'll take these folks through . . . to where they're goin'."

"I'm no wagon master," Fury said.

"You know the frontier," Crofton insisted. Anger gave him strength, made him rally enough to lift his head from the ground and glare at Fury. "You can get 'em through. I know you can."

"Don't excite him," warned the gray-haired doctor.

"Why the hell not?" Fury snapped, glancing up at the physician. He noticed now that the man had his arm around the shoulders of a pretty red-headed girl in her teens, probably his daughter. He went on, "What harm's it going to do?"

The girl exclaimed, "Oh! How can you be so . . . so callous?"

Crofton said, "Fury's just bein' practical, Carrie. He knows we got to . . . got to hash this out now. Only chance we'll get." He looked at Fury again. "I can't make you promise, but it . . . it'd sure set my mind at ease while I'm passin' over if I knew you'd take care of these folks."

Fury sighed. It was rare for him to promise anything to anybody. Giving your word was a quick way of getting in over your head in somebody else's problems. But Crofton was dying, and even though they had never crossed

179

paths before. Fury recognized in the old man a fellow Westerner.

"All right," he said.

A little shudder ran through Crofton's battered body, and he rested his head back against the grassy ground. "Thanks," he said, the word gusting out of him along with a ragged breath.

"Where are you headed?" Fury figured the immigrants could tell him, but he wanted to hear the destination from Crofton.

"Colorado Territory . . . Folks figure to start 'em a town . . . somewhere on the South Platte. Won't be hard for you to find . . . a good place."

No, it wouldn't, Fury thought. No wagon train journey could be called easy, but at least this one wouldn't have to deal with crossing mountains, just prairie. Prairie filled with savages and outlaws, that is.

A grim smile plucked at Fury's mouth as that thought crossed his mind. "Anything else you need to tell me?" he asked Crofton.

The wagonmaster shook his head and let his eyelids slide closed. "Nope. Figger I'll rest a spell now. We can talk again later."

"Sure," Fury said softly, knowing that in all likelihood, Leander Crofton would never wake up from this rest.

Less than a minute later, Crofton coughed suddenly, a wracking sound. His head twisted to the side, and blood welled for a few seconds from the corner of his mouth. Fury heard some of the women in the crowd cry out and turn away, and he suspected some of the men did, too.

"Well, that's all," he said, straightening easily from his kneeling position beside Crofton's body. He looked at the doctor. The red-headed teenager had her face pressed to the front of her father's shirt and her shoulders were shaking

180

with sobs. She wasn't the only one crying, and even the ones who were dry-eyed still looked plenty grim.

"We'll have a funeral service as soon as a grave is dug," said the doctor. "Then I suppose we'll be moving on. You should know, Mr. . . . Fury, was it? You should know that none of us will hold you to that promise you made to Mr. Crofton."

Fury shrugged. "Didn't ask if you intended to or not. I'm the one who made the promise. Reckon I'll keep it."

He saw surprise on some of the faces watching him. All of these travelers had probably figured him for some sort of drifter. Well, that was fair enough. Drifting was what he did best.

But that didn't mean he was a man who ignored promises. He had given his word, and there was no way he could back out now.

He met the startled stare of the doctor and went on, "Who's the captain here? You?"

"No, I . . . You see, we hadn't gotten around to electing a captain yet. We only left Independence a couple of weeks ago, and we were all happy with the leadership of Mr. Crofton. We didn't see the need to select a captain."

Crofton should have insisted on it, Fury thought with a grimace. You never could tell when trouble would pop up. Crofton's body lying on the ground was grisly proof of that.

Fury looked around at the crowd. From the number of people standing there, he figured most of the wagons in the train were at least represented in this gathering. Lifting his voice, he said, "You all heard what Crofton asked me to do. I gave him my word I'd take over this wagon train and get it on through to Colorado Territory. Anybody got any objection to that?"

His gaze moved over the faces of the men and women who were standing and looking silently back at him. The

181

silence was awkward and heavy. No one was objecting, but Fury could tell they weren't too happy with this unexpected turn of events.

Well, he thought, when he had rolled out of his soogans that morning, he hadn't expected to be in charge of a wagon train full of strangers before the day was over.

The gray-haired doctor was the first one to find his voice. "We can't speak for everyone on the train, Mr. Fury," he said. "But I don't know you, sir, and I have some reservations about turning over the welfare of my daughter and myself to a total stranger."

Several others in the crowd nodded in agreement with the sentiment expressed by the physician.

"Crofton knew me."

"He knew you to have a reputation as some sort of gunman!"

Fury took a deep breath and wished to hell he had come along after Crofton was already dead. Then he wouldn't be saddled with a pledge to take care of these people.

"I'm not wanted by the law," he said. "That's more than a lot of men out here on the frontier can say, especially those who have been here for as long as I have. Like I said, I'm not looking to cause trouble. I was riding along and minding my own business when I came across you people. There's too many of you for me to fight. You want to start out toward Colorado on your own, I can't stop you. But you're going to have to learn a hell of a lot in a hurry."

"What do you mean by that?"

Fury smiled grimly. "For one thing, if you stop spread out like this, you're making a target of yourselves for every Indian in these parts who wants a few fresh scalps for his lodge." He looked pointedly at the long red hair of the doctor's daughter. Carrie—that was what Crofton had called her, Fury remembered.

182

Her father paled a little, and another man said, "I didn't think there was any Indians this far east." Other murmurs of concern came from the crowd.

Fury knew he had gotten through to them. But before any of them had a chance to say that he should honor his promise to Crofton and take over, the sound of hoofbeats made him turn quickly.

A man was riding hard toward the wagon train from the west, leaning over the neck of his horse and urging it on to greater speed. The brim of his hat was blown back by the wind of his passage, and Fury saw anxious, dark brown features underneath it. The newcomer galloped up to the crowd gathered next to the lead wagon, hauled his lathered mount to a halt, and dropped lithely from the saddle. His eyes went wide with shock when he saw Crofton's body on the ground, and then his gaze flicked to Fury.

"You son of a bitch!" he howled.

And his hand darted toward the gun holstered on his hip.

If you enjoyed this book, subscribe now and get...

TWO FREE

A $7.00 VALUE–

If you would like to read more of the very best, most exciting, adventurous, action-packed Westerns being published today, you'll want to subscribe to True Value's Western Home Subscription Service.

Each month the editors of True Value will select the 6 very best Westerns from America's leading publishers for special readers like you. You'll be able to preview these new titles as soon as they are published, *FREE* for ten days with no obligation!

TWO FREE BOOKS

When you subscribe, we'll send you your first month's shipment of the newest and best 6 Westerns for you to preview. With your first shipment, two of these books will be yours as our introductory gift to you absolutely *FREE* (a $7.00 value), regardless of what you decide to do. If

you like them, as much as we think you will, keep all six books but pay for just 4 at the low subscriber rate of just $2.75 each. If you decide to return them, keep 2 of the titles as our gift. No obligation.

Special Subscriber Savings

When you become a True Value subscriber you'll save money several ways. First, all regular monthly selections will be billed at the low subscriber price of just $2.75 each. That's at least a savings of $4.50 each month below the publishers price. Second, there is never any shipping, handling or other hidden charges—*Free home delivery*. What's more there is no minimum number of books you must buy, you may return any selection for full credit and you can cancel your subscription at any time. A TRUE VALUE!